A LUCKY LUKE ADVENTURE

UNDER A WESTERN SKY

MORRIS

9th CINEBOOK
The 9th Art Publisher

Original title: Sous Le Ciel De L'ouest

Original edition: © Dupuis 1952 by Morris
© Lucky Comics
www.lucky-luke.com

English translation: © 2015 Cinebook Ltd

Translator: Jerome Saincantin
Lettering and text layout: Design Amorandi
Printed in Spain by EGEDSA

This edition first published in Great Britain in 2015 by
Cinebook Ltd
56 Beech Avenue
Canterbury, Kent
CT4 7TA
www.cinebook.com

A CIP catalogue record for this book
is available from the British Library

ISBN 978-1-84918-273-7

9th CINEBOOK
The 9th Art Publisher

The Return of TRIGGER JOE

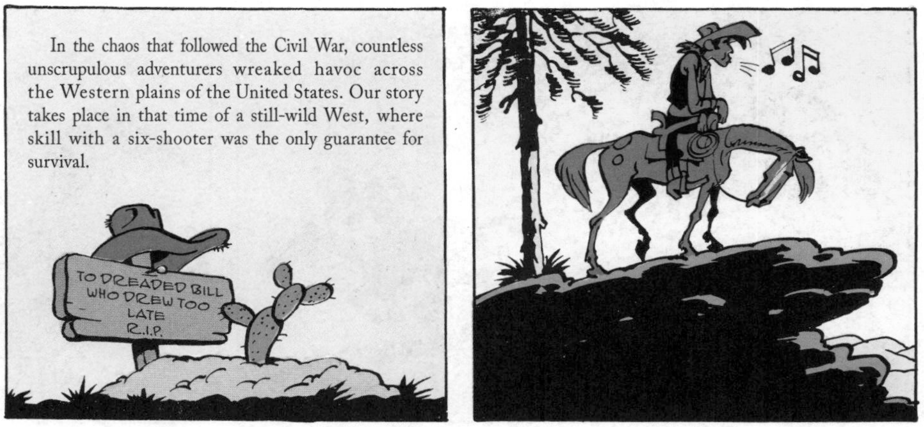
In the chaos that followed the Civil War, countless unscrupulous adventurers wreaked havoc across the Western plains of the United States. Our story takes place in that time of a still-wild West, where skill with a six-shooter was the only guarantee for survival.
TO DREADED BILL WHO DREW TOO LATE R.I.P.

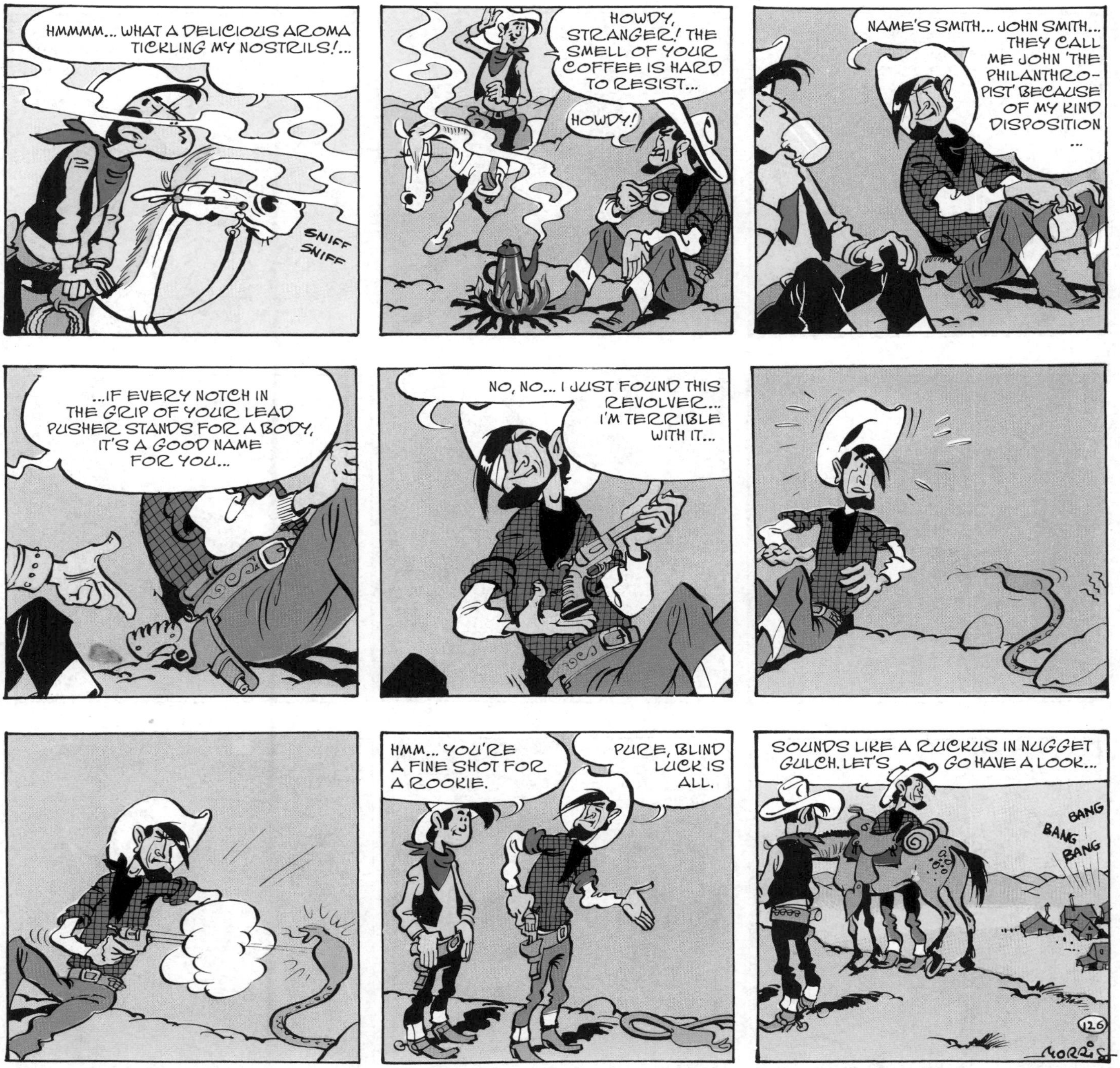
HMMMM... WHAT A DELICIOUS AROMA TICKLING MY NOSTRILS!...
SNIFF SNIFF
HOWDY, STRANGER! THE SMELL OF YOUR COFFEE IS HARD TO RESIST...
HOWDY!
NAME'S SMITH... JOHN SMITH... THEY CALL ME JOHN 'THE PHILANTHRO-PIST' BECAUSE OF MY KIND DISPOSITION ...
...IF EVERY NOTCH IN THE GRIP OF YOUR LEAD PUSHER STANDS FOR A BODY, IT'S A GOOD NAME FOR YOU...
NO, NO... I JUST FOUND THIS REVOLVER... I'M TERRIBLE WITH IT...
HMM... YOU'RE A FINE SHOT FOR A ROOKIE.
PURE, BLIND LUCK IS ALL.
SOUNDS LIKE A RUCKUS IN NUGGET GULCH. LET'S GO HAVE A LOOK...
BANG
BANG
BANG
126
MORRIS

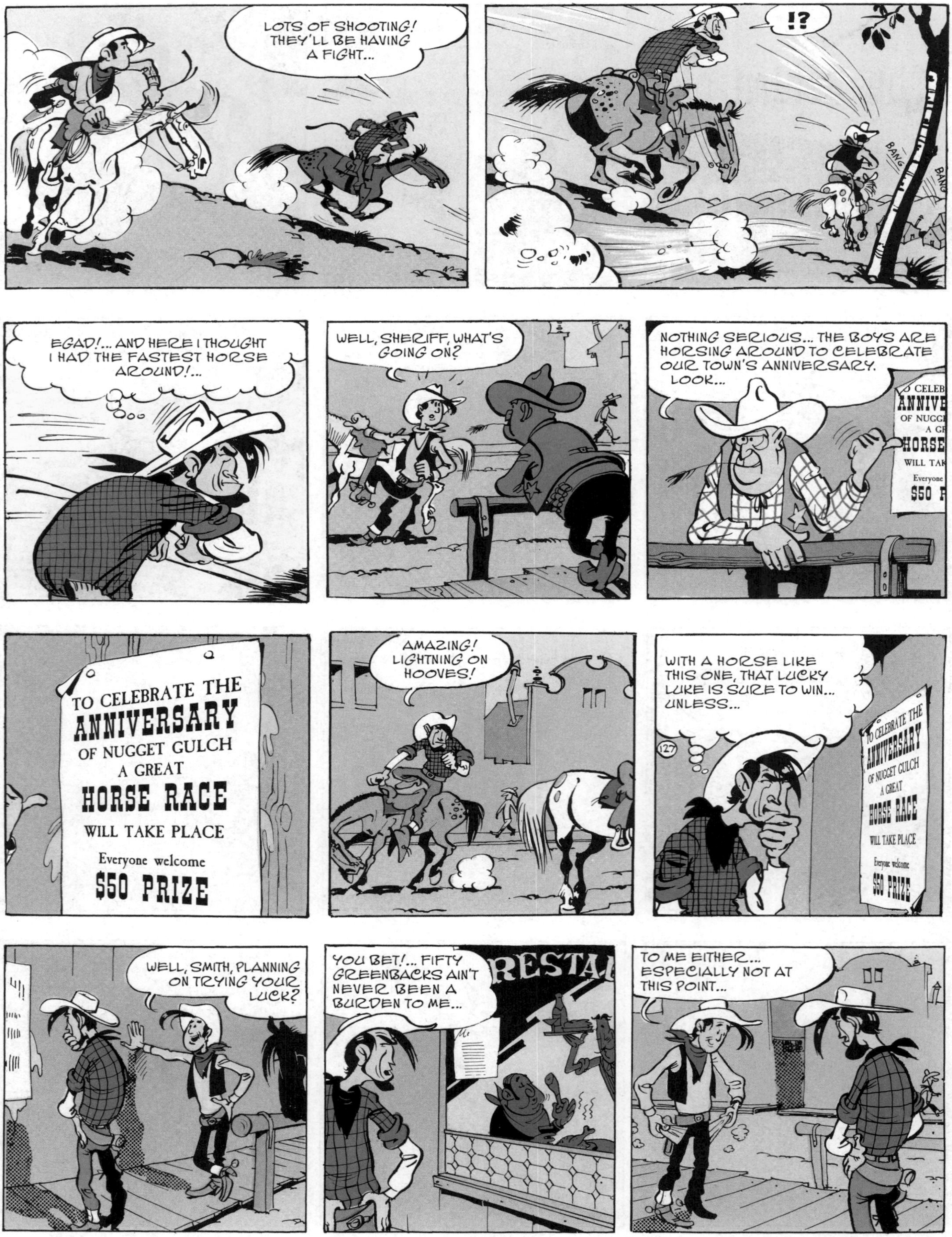
LOTS OF SHOOTING! THEY'LL BE HAVING A FIGHT...
!?
BANG
BANG
EGAD!... AND HERE I THOUGHT I HAD THE FASTEST HORSE AROUND!...
WELL, SHERIFF, WHAT'S GOING ON?
NOTHING SERIOUS... THE BOYS ARE HORSING AROUND TO CELEBRATE OUR TOWN'S ANNIVERSARY. LOOK...
TO CELEBRATE THE ANNIVERSARY OF NUGGET GULCH A GREAT HORSE RACE WILL TAKE PLACE Everyone welcome $50 PRIZE
AMAZING! LIGHTNING ON HOOVES!
WITH A HORSE LIKE THIS ONE, THAT LUCKY LUKE IS SURE TO WIN... UNLESS...
WELL, SMITH, PLANNING ON TRYING YOUR LUCK?
YOU BET!... FIFTY GREENBACKS AIN'T NEVER BEEN A BURDEN TO ME...
RESTA
TO ME EITHER... ESPECIALLY NOT AT THIS POINT...

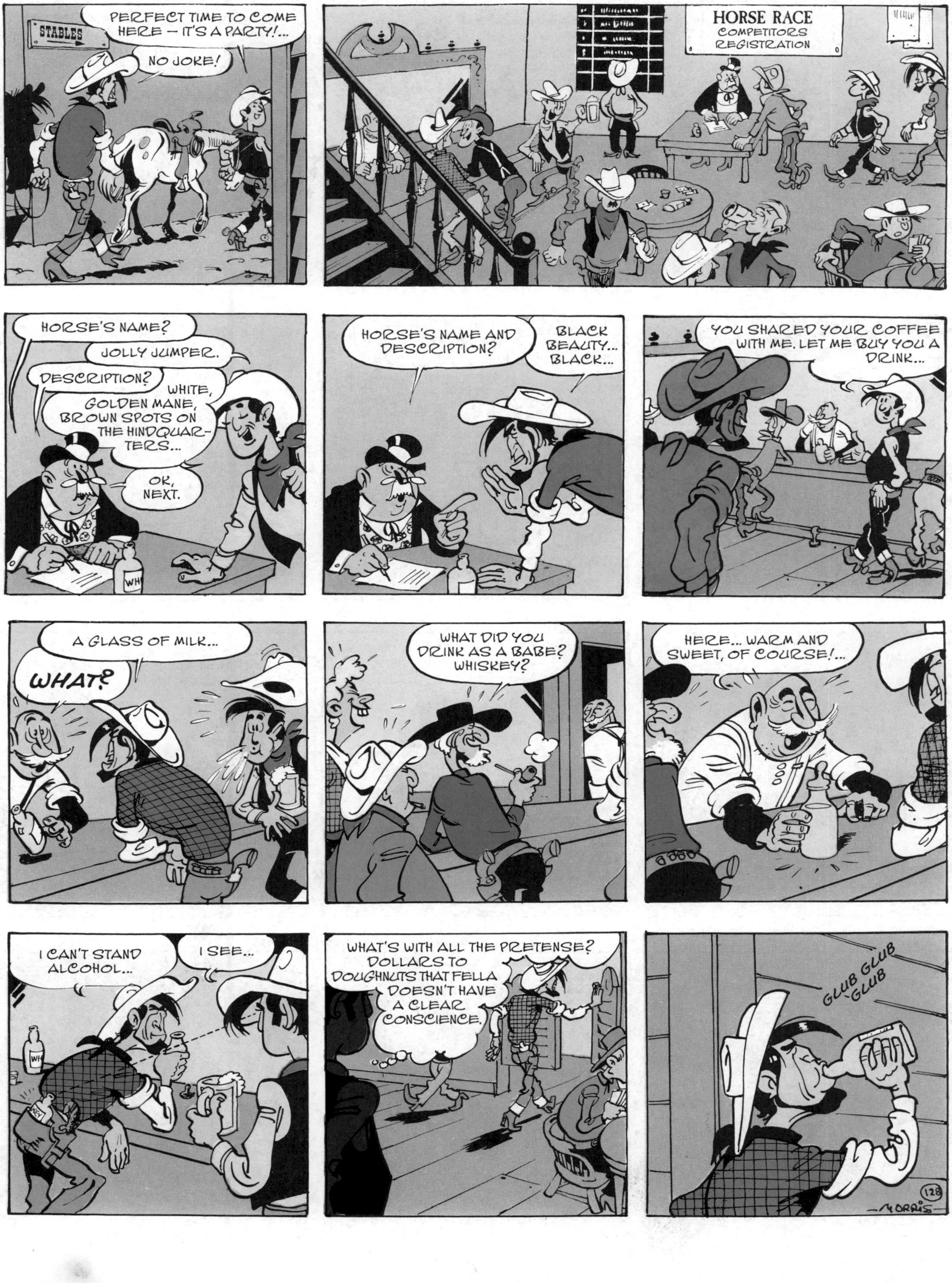

STABLES
PERFECT TIME TO COME HERE – IT'S A PARTY!...
NO JOKE!
HORSE RACE
COMPETITORS REGISTRATION
HORSE'S NAME?
JOLLY JUMPER.
DESCRIPTION?
WHITE, GOLDEN MANE, BROWN SPOTS ON THE HINDQUARTERS...
OK, NEXT.
HORSE'S NAME AND DESCRIPTION?
BLACK BEAUTY... BLACK...
YOU SHARED YOUR COFFEE WITH ME. LET ME BUY YOU A DRINK...
A GLASS OF MILK...
WHAT?
WHAT DID YOU DRINK AS A BABE? WHISKEY?
HERE... WARM AND SWEET, OF COURSE!...
I CAN'T STAND ALCOHOL...
I SEE...
WHAT'S WITH ALL THE PRETENSE? DOLLARS TO DOUGHNUTS THAT FELLA DOESN'T HAVE A CLEAR CONSCIENCE.
GLUB GLUB GLUB
128
MORRIS

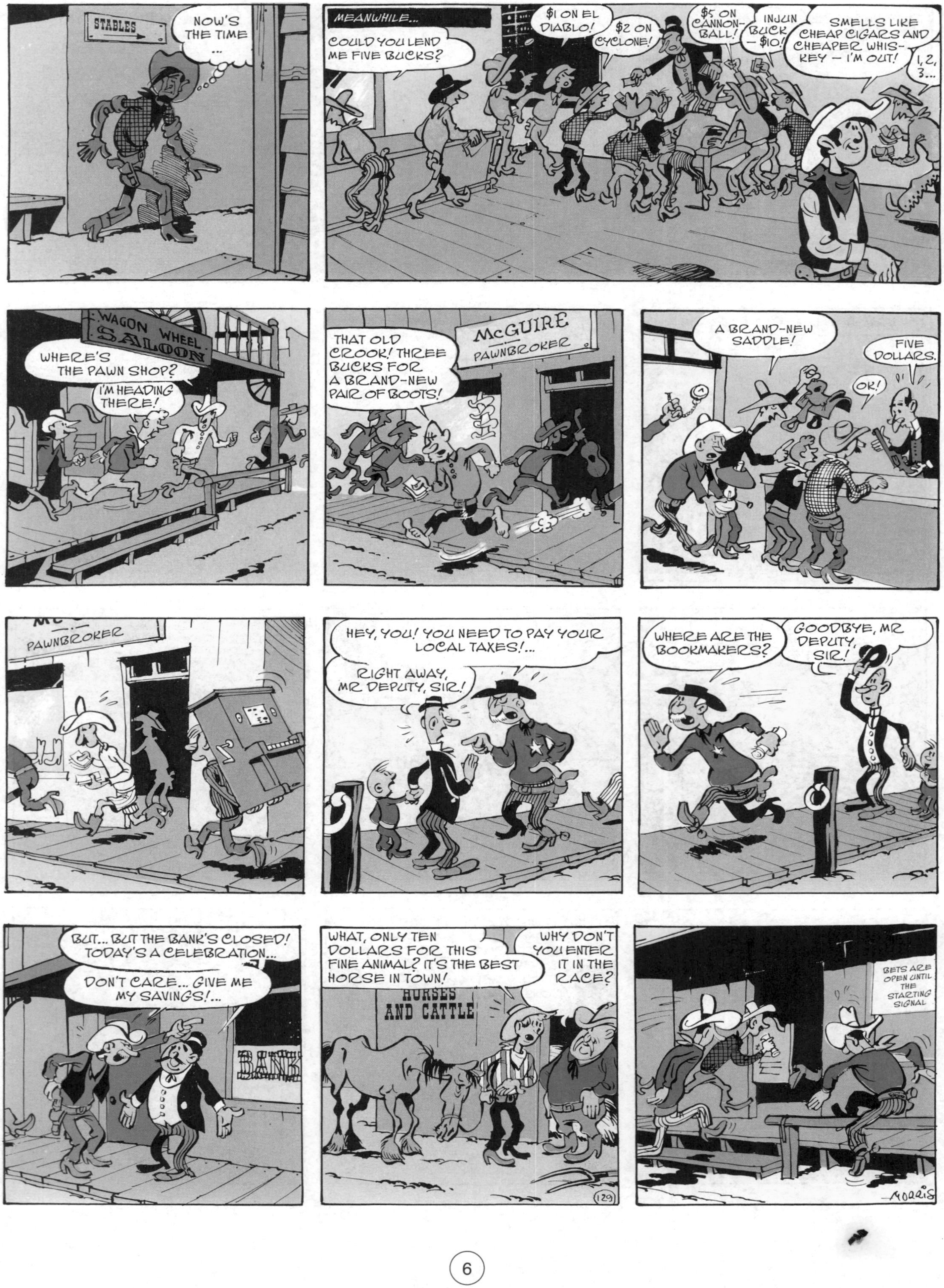
STABLES
NOW'S THE TIME ...
MEANWHILE...
COULD YOU LEND ME FIVE BUCKS?
$1 ON EL DIABLO!
$2 ON CYCLONE!
$5 ON CANNON-BALL!
INJUN BUCK – $10!
SMELLS LIKE CHEAP CIGARS AND CHEAPER WHIS-KEY – I'M OUT!
1, 2, 3...
WAGON WHEEL SALOON
WHERE'S THE PAWN SHOP?
I'M HEADING THERE!
McGUIRE PAWNBROKER
THAT OLD CROOK! THREE BUCKS FOR A BRAND-NEW PAIR OF BOOTS!
A BRAND-NEW SADDLE!
FIVE DOLLARS.
OK!
PAWNBROKER
HEY, YOU! YOU NEED TO PAY YOUR LOCAL TAXES!...
RIGHT AWAY, MR DEPUTY, SIR!
WHERE ARE THE BOOKMAKERS?
GOODBYE, MR DEPUTY, SIR!
BUT... BUT THE BANK'S CLOSED! TODAY'S A CELEBRATION...
DON'T CARE... GIVE ME MY SAVINGS!...
BANK
WHAT, ONLY TEN DOLLARS FOR THIS FINE ANIMAL? IT'S THE BEST HORSE IN TOWN!
WHY DON'T YOU ENTER IT IN THE RACE?
HORSES AND CATTLE
(129)
BETS ARE OPEN UNTIL THE STARTING SIGNAL
MORRIS

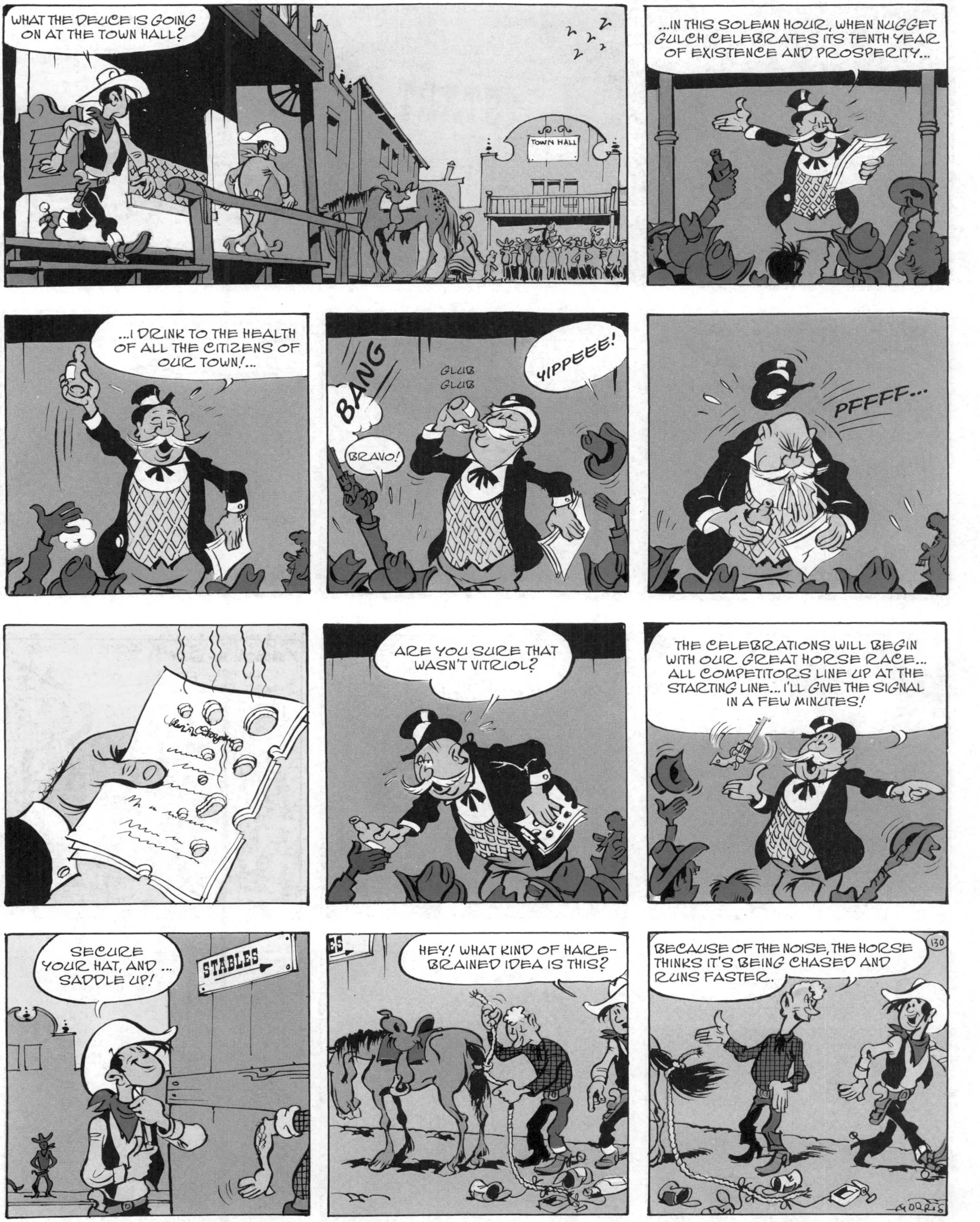
WHAT THE DEUCE IS GOING ON AT THE TOWN HALL?
Z Z Z Z Z
TOWN HALL
...IN THIS SOLEMN HOUR, WHEN NUGGET GULCH CELEBRATES ITS TENTH YEAR OF EXISTENCE AND PROSPERITY...
...I DRINK TO THE HEALTH OF ALL THE CITIZENS OF OUR TOWN!...
BANG
GLUB GLUB
YIPPEEE!
BRAVO!
PFFFF...
ARE YOU SURE THAT WASN'T VITRIOL?
THE CELEBRATIONS WILL BEGIN WITH OUR GREAT HORSE RACE... ALL COMPETITORS LINE UP AT THE STARTING LINE... I'LL GIVE THE SIGNAL IN A FEW MINUTES!
SECURE YOUR HAT, AND ... SADDLE UP!
STABLES
HEY! WHAT KIND OF HARE-BRAINED IDEA IS THIS?
BECAUSE OF THE NOISE, THE HORSE THINKS IT'S BEING CHASED AND RUNS FASTER.
130
MORRIS

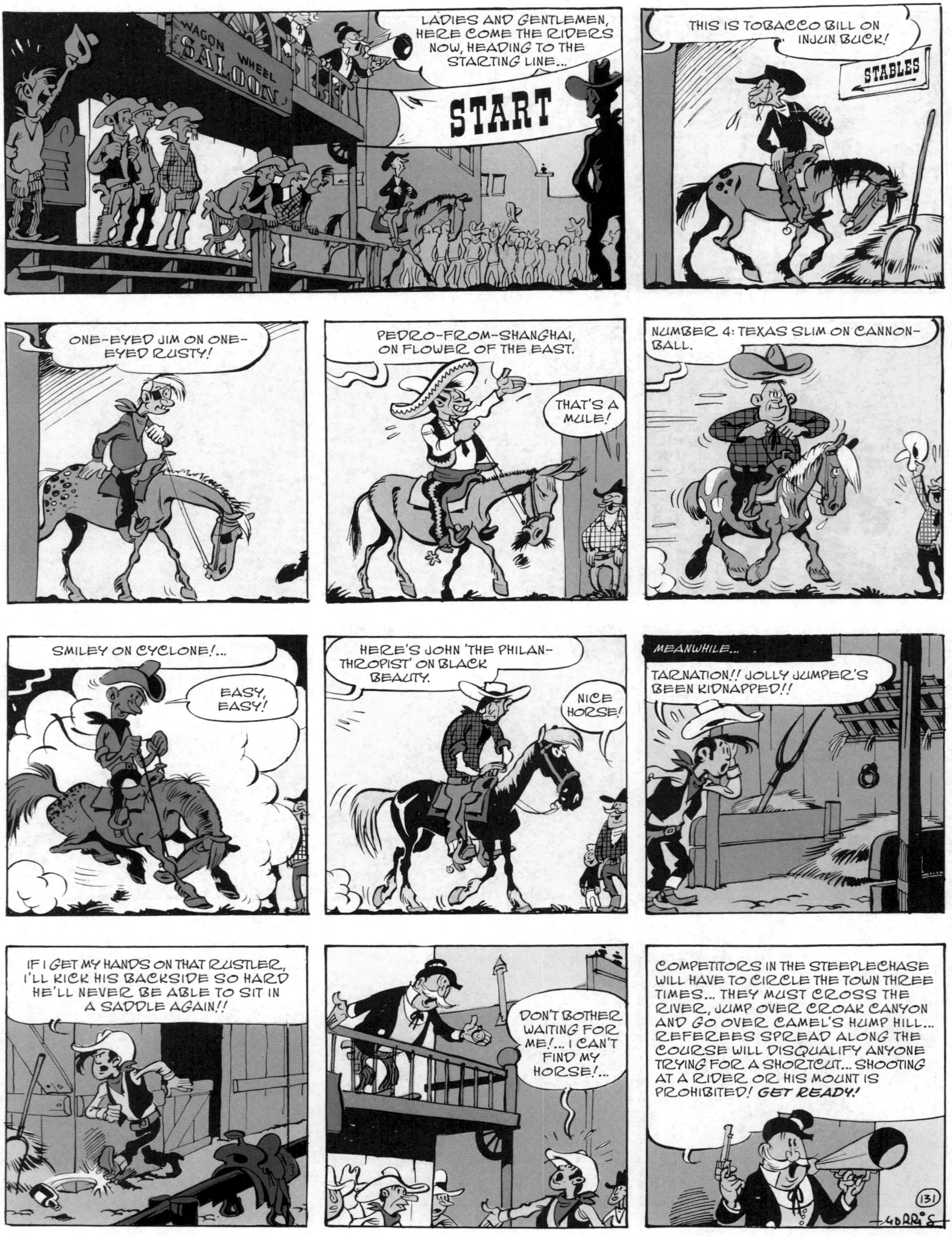

WAGON WHEEL SALOON
LADIES AND GENTLEMEN, HERE COME THE RIDERS NOW, HEADING TO THE STARTING LINE...
START
THIS IS TOBACCO BILL ON INJUN BUCK!
STABLES
ONE-EYED JIM ON ONE-EYED RUSTY!
PEDRO-FROM-SHANGHAI, ON FLOWER OF THE EAST.
THAT'S A MULE!
NUMBER 4: TEXAS SLIM ON CANNON-BALL.
SMILEY ON CYCLONE!...
EASY, EASY!
HERE'S JOHN 'THE PHILAN-THROPIST' ON BLACK BEAUTY.
NICE HORSE!
MEANWHILE...
TARNATION!! JOLLY JUMPER'S BEEN KIDNAPPED!!
IF I GET MY HANDS ON THAT RUSTLER, I'LL KICK HIS BACKSIDE SO HARD HE'LL NEVER BE ABLE TO SIT IN A SADDLE AGAIN!!
DON'T BOTHER WAITING FOR ME!... I CAN'T FIND MY HORSE!...
COMPETITORS IN THE STEEPLECHASE WILL HAVE TO CIRCLE THE TOWN THREE TIMES... THEY MUST CROSS THE RIVER, JUMP OVER CROAK CANYON AND GO OVER CAMEL'S HUMP HILL... REFEREES SPREAD ALONG THE COURSE WILL DISQUALIFY ANYONE TRYING FOR A SHORTCUT... SHOOTING AT A RIDER OR HIS MOUNT IS PROHIBITED! GET READY!
131
MORRIS

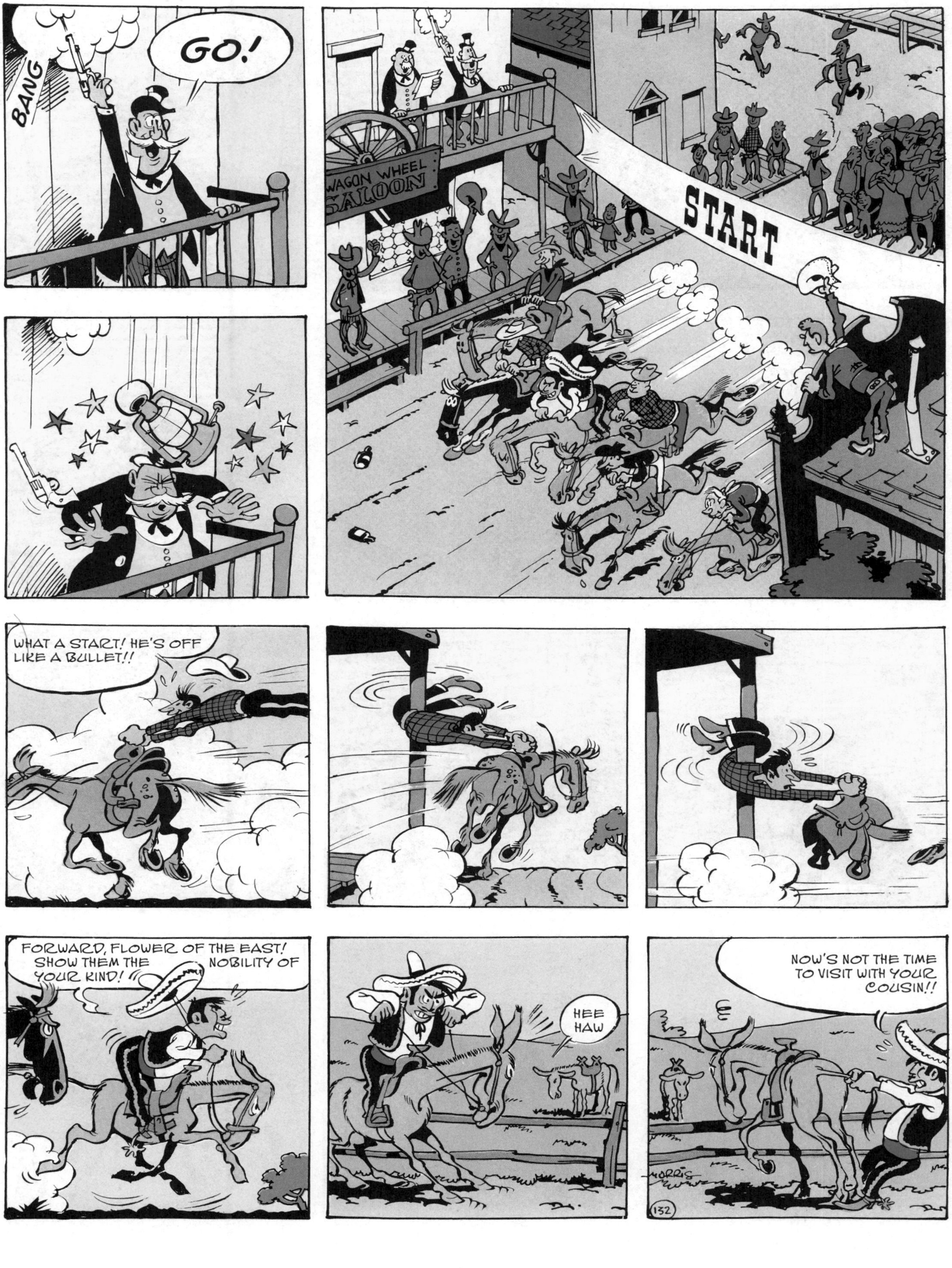
BANG
GO!
WAGON WHEEL SALOON
START
WHAT A START! HE'S OFF LIKE A BULLET!!
FORWARD, FLOWER OF THE EAST! SHOW THEM THE NOBILITY OF YOUR KIND!
HEE HAW
NOW'S NOT THE TIME TO VISIT WITH YOUR COUSIN!!
MORRIS
132

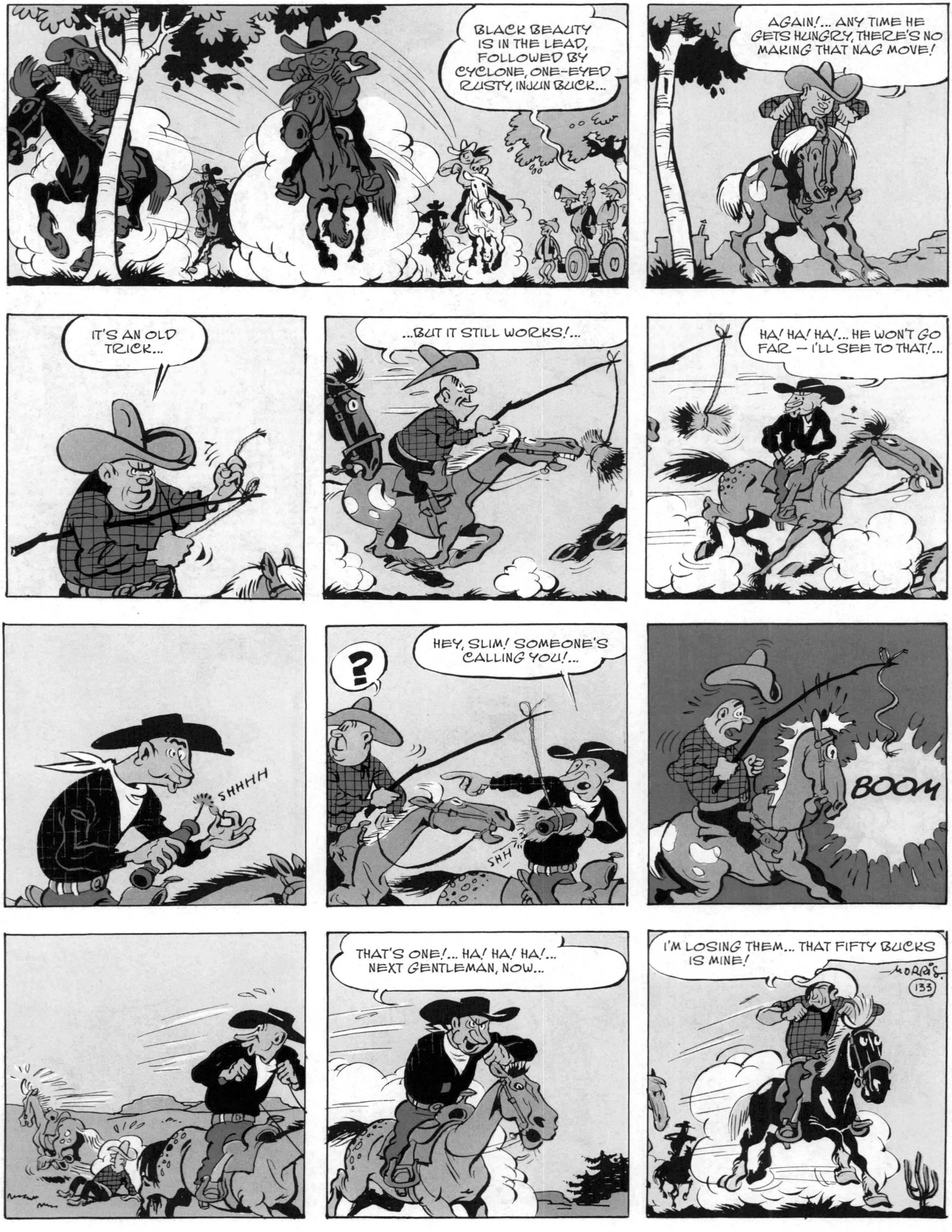
BLACK BEAUTY IS IN THE LEAD, FOLLOWED BY CYCLONE, ONE-EYED RUSTY, INJUN BUCK...
AGAIN!... ANY TIME HE GETS HUNGRY, THERE'S NO MAKING THAT NAG MOVE!
IT'S AN OLD TRICK...
...BUT IT STILL WORKS!...
HA! HA! HA!... HE WON'T GO FAR – I'LL SEE TO THAT!...
SHHHH
?
HEY, SLIM! SOMEONE'S CALLING YOU!...
SHH
BOOM
THAT'S ONE!... HA! HA! HA!... NEXT GENTLEMAN, NOW...
I'M LOSING THEM... THAT FIFTY BUCKS IS MINE!
MORRIS
133

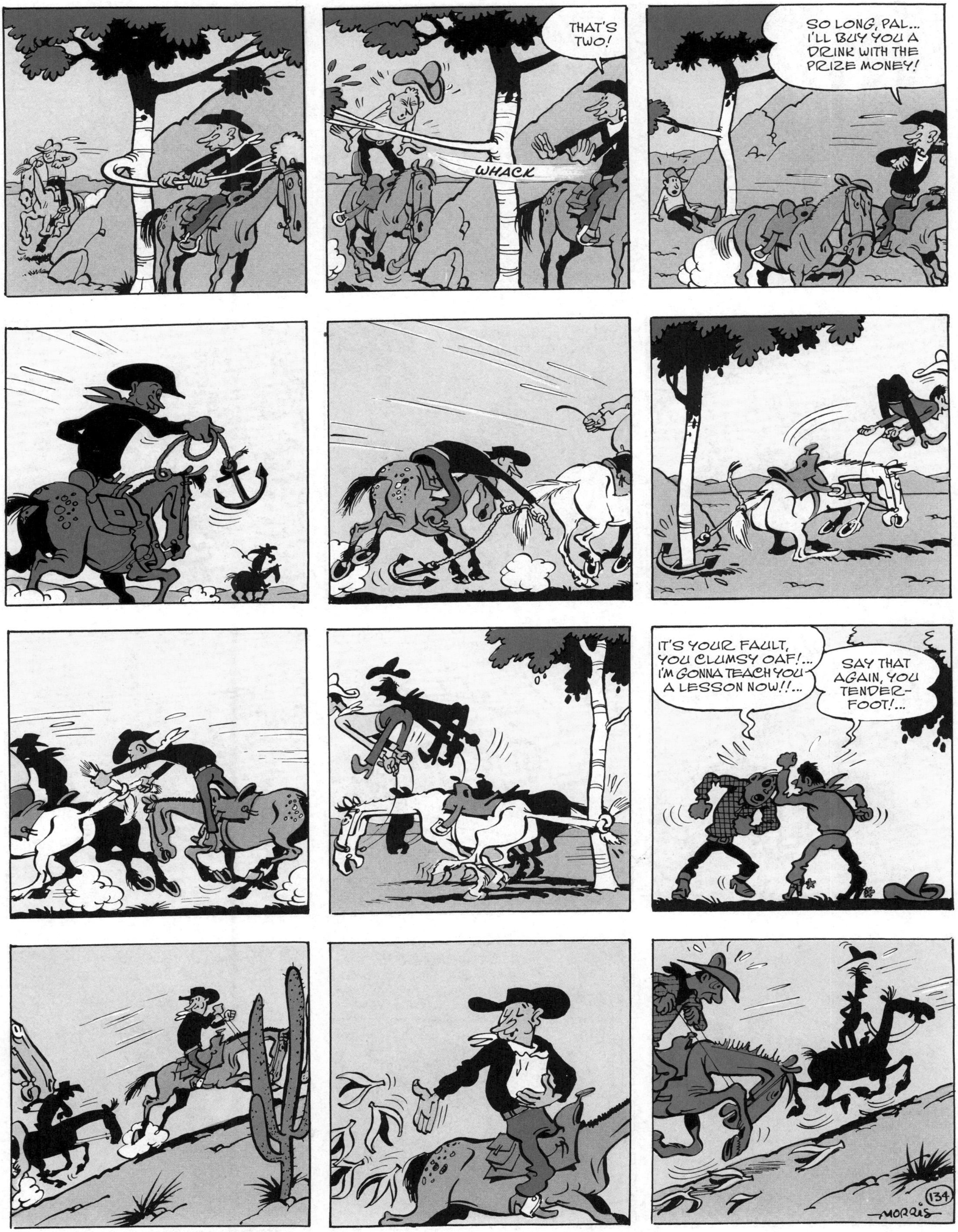
THAT'S TWO!
WHACK
SO LONG, PAL... I'LL BUY YOU A DRINK WITH THE PRIZE MONEY!
IT'S YOUR FAULT, YOU CLUMSY OAF!... I'M GONNA TEACH YOU A LESSON NOW!!...
SAY THAT AGAIN, YOU TENDER-FOOT!...
134
MORRIS

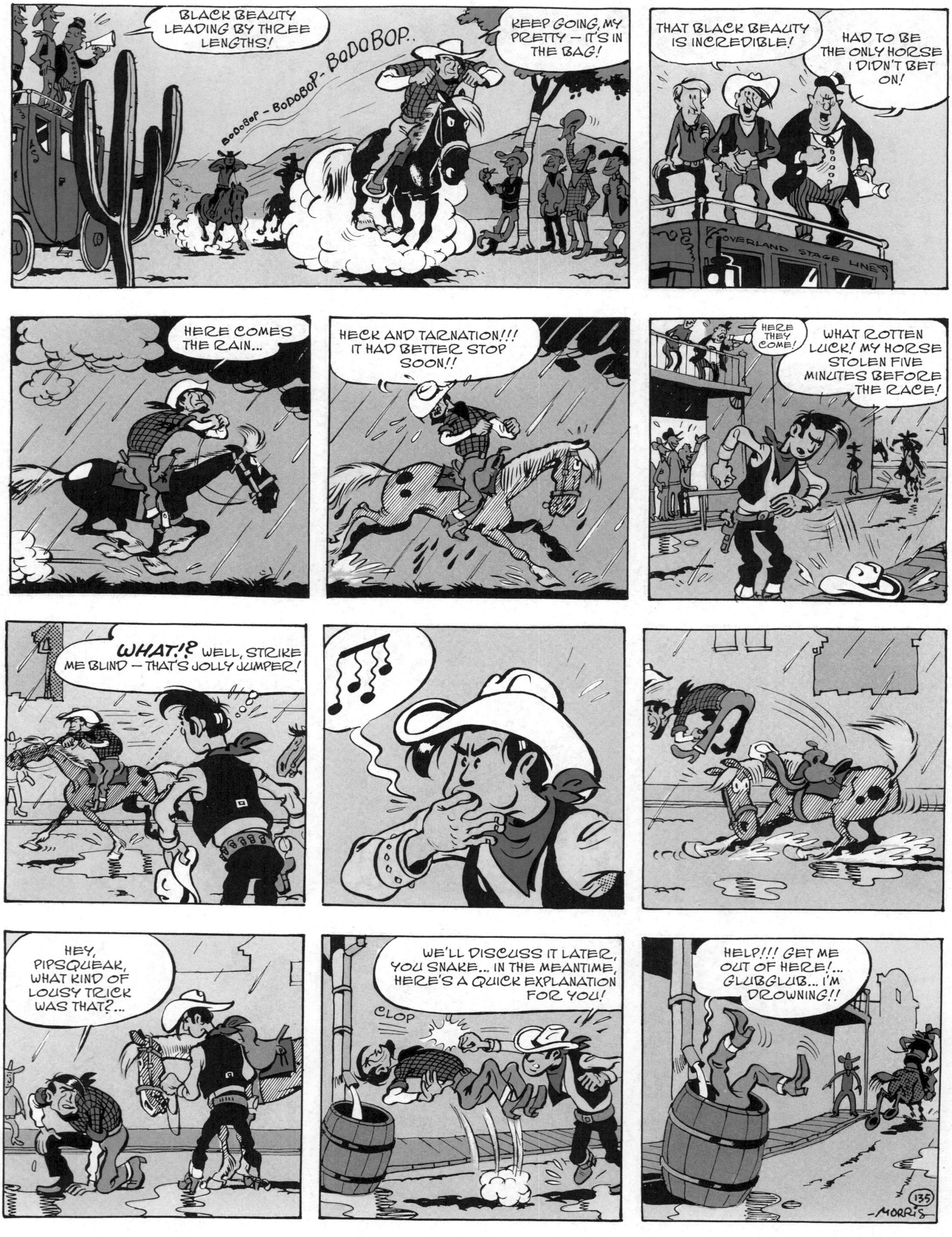
BLACK BEAUTY LEADING BY THREE LENGTHS!
BODOBOP - BODOBOP - BODOBOP..
KEEP GOING, MY PRETTY – IT'S IN THE BAG!
THAT BLACK BEAUTY IS INCREDIBLE!
HAD TO BE THE ONLY HORSE I DIDN'T BET ON!
OVERLAND STAGE LINE
HERE COMES THE RAIN...
HECK AND TARNATION!!! IT HAD BETTER STOP SOON!!
HERE THEY COME!
WHAT ROTTEN LUCK! MY HORSE STOLEN FIVE MINUTES BEFORE THE RACE!
WHAT!? WELL, STRIKE ME BLIND – THAT'S JOLLY JUMPER!
HEY, PIPSQUEAK, WHAT KIND OF LOUSY TRICK WAS THAT?...
WE'LL DISCUSS IT LATER, YOU SNAKE... IN THE MEANTIME, HERE'S A QUICK EXPLANATION FOR YOU!
CLOP
HELP!!! GET ME OUT OF HERE!... GLUBGLUB... I'M DROWNING!!
135
MORRIS

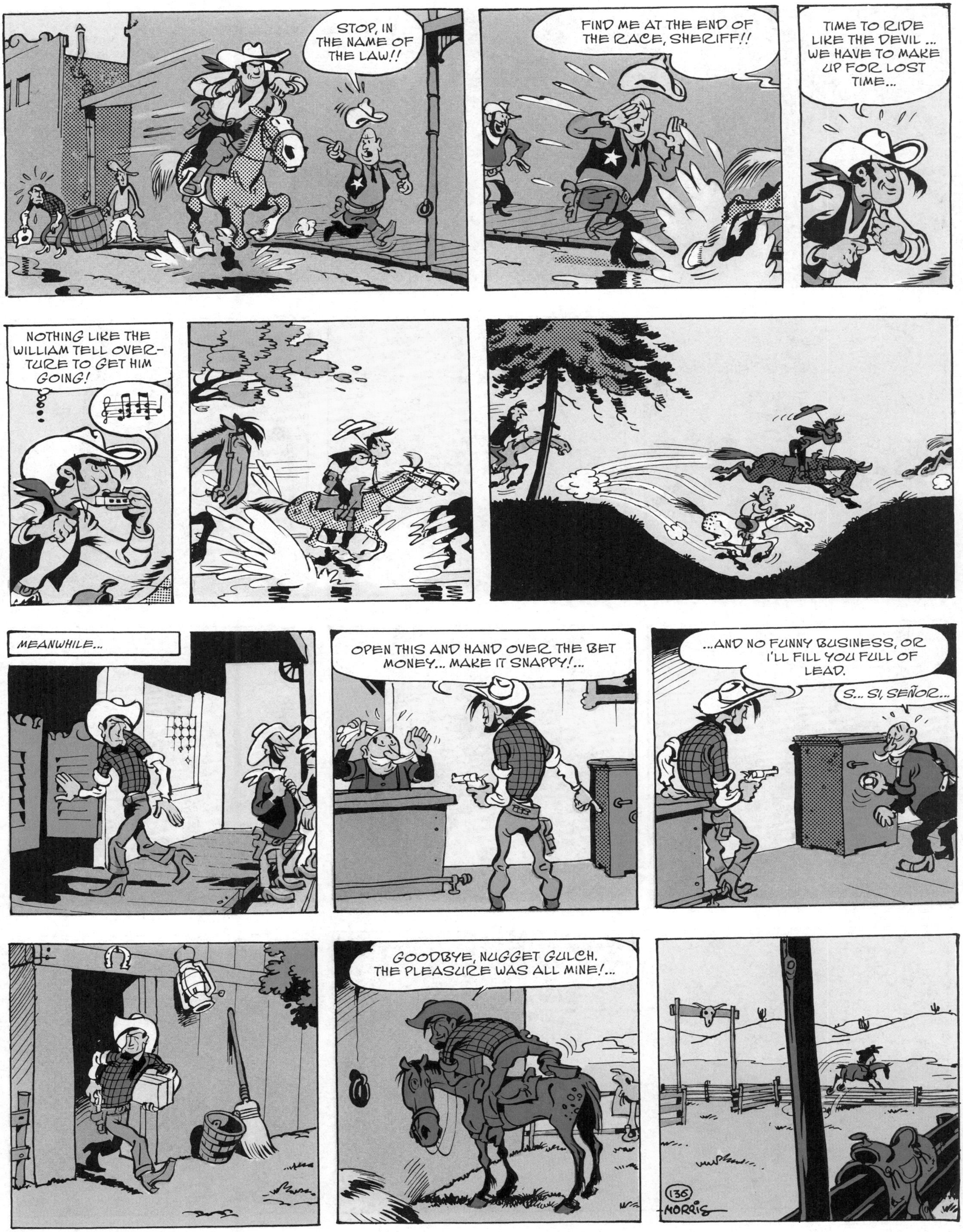
STOP, IN THE NAME OF THE LAW!!
FIND ME AT THE END OF THE RACE, SHERIFF!!
TIME TO RIDE LIKE THE DEVIL ... WE HAVE TO MAKE UP FOR LOST TIME...
NOTHING LIKE THE WILLIAM TELL OVERTURE TO GET HIM GOING!
MEANWHILE...
OPEN THIS AND HAND OVER THE BET MONEY... MAKE IT SNAPPY!...
...AND NO FUNNY BUSINESS, OR I'LL FILL YOU FULL OF LEAD.
S... SI, SEÑOR...
GOODBYE, NUGGET GULCH. THE PLEASURE WAS ALL MINE!...
136
MORRIS

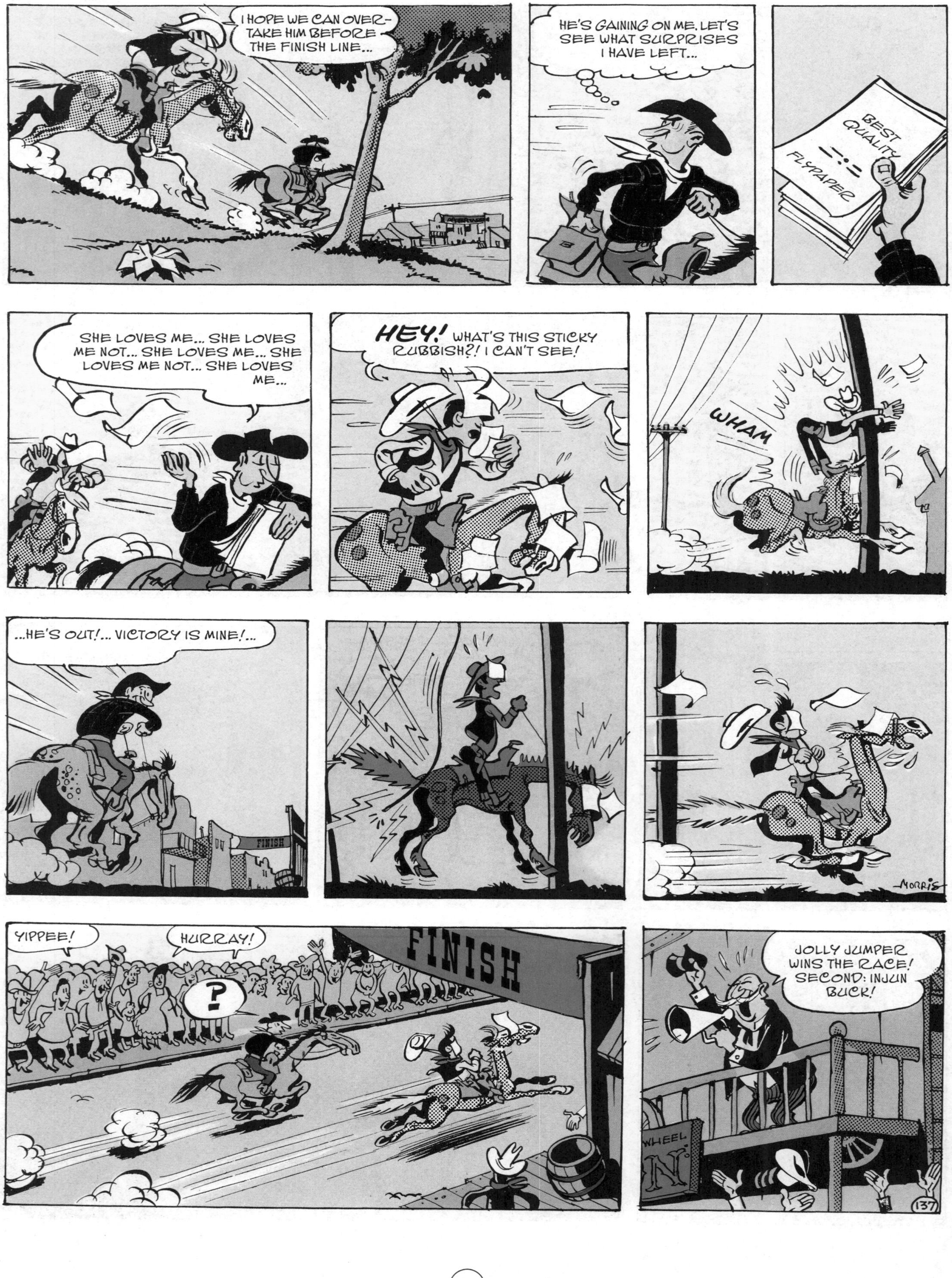
I HOPE WE CAN OVER-TAKE HIM BEFORE THE FINISH LINE...
HE'S GAINING ON ME. LET'S SEE WHAT SURPRISES I HAVE LEFT...
BEST QUALITY FLYPAPER
SHE LOVES ME... SHE LOVES ME NOT... SHE LOVES ME... SHE LOVES ME NOT... SHE LOVES ME...
HEY! WHAT'S THIS STICKY RUBBISH?! I CAN'T SEE!
WHAM
...HE'S OUT!... VICTORY IS MINE!...
FINISH
MORRIS
YIPPEE!
HURRAY!
FINISH
?
JOLLY JUMPER WINS THE RACE! SECOND: INJUN BUCK!
WHEEL
137

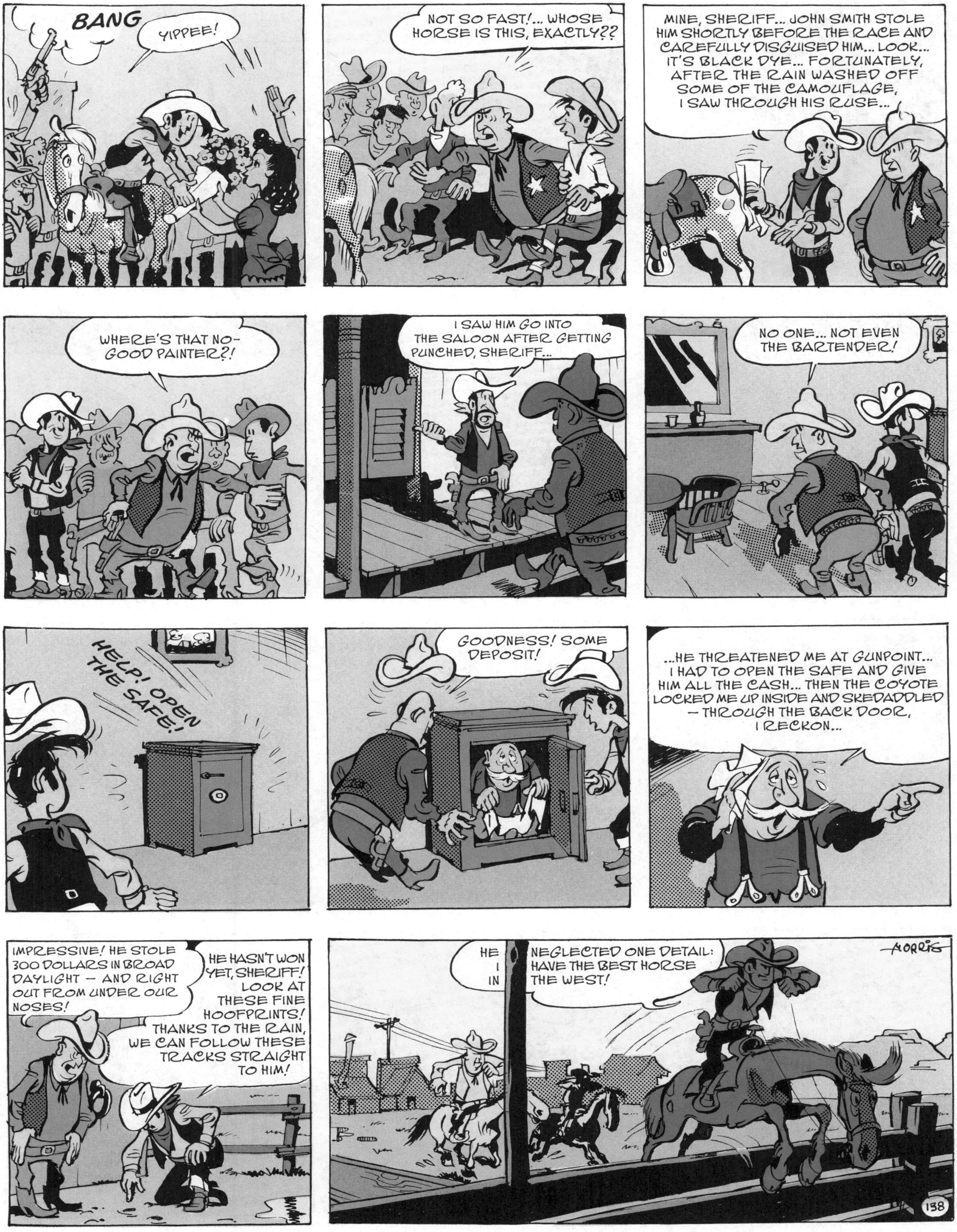
BANG
YIPPEE!
NOT SO FAST!... WHOSE HORSE IS THIS, EXACTLY??
MINE, SHERIFF... JOHN SMITH STOLE HIM SHORTLY BEFORE THE RACE AND CAREFULLY DISGUISED HIM... LOOK... IT'S BLACK DYE... FORTUNATELY, AFTER THE RAIN WASHED OFF SOME OF THE CAMOUFLAGE, I SAW THROUGH HIS RUSE...
WHERE'S THAT NO-GOOD PAINTER?!
I SAW HIM GO INTO THE SALOON AFTER GETTING PUNCHED, SHERIFF...
NO ONE... NOT EVEN THE BARTENDER!
HELP! OPEN THE SAFE!
GOODNESS! SOME DEPOSIT!
...HE THREATENED ME AT GUNPOINT... I HAD TO OPEN THE SAFE AND GIVE HIM ALL THE CASH... THEN THE COYOTE LOCKED ME UP INSIDE AND SKEDADDLED – THROUGH THE BACK DOOR, I RECKON...
IMPRESSIVE! HE STOLE 300 DOLLARS IN BROAD DAYLIGHT – AND RIGHT OUT FROM UNDER OUR NOSES!
HE HASN'T WON YET, SHERIFF! LOOK AT THESE FINE HOOFPRINTS! THANKS TO THE RAIN, WE CAN FOLLOW THESE TRACKS STRAIGHT TO HIM!
HE NEGLECTED ONE DETAIL: I HAVE THE BEST HORSE IN THE WEST!
MORRIS
138

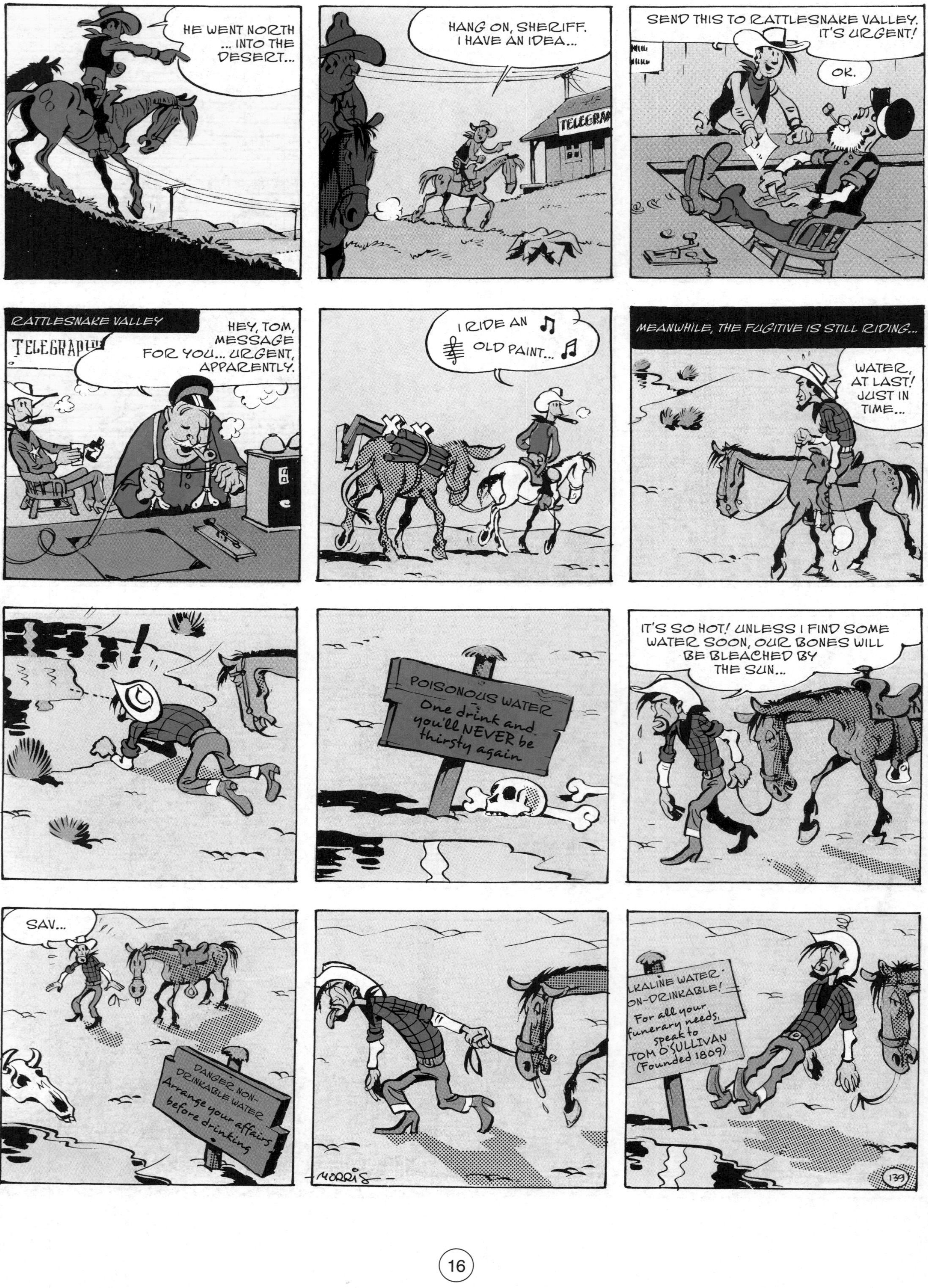
HE WENT NORTH ... INTO THE DESERT...
HANG ON, SHERIFF. I HAVE AN IDEA...
TELEGRAP
SEND THIS TO RATTLESNAKE VALLEY. IT'S URGENT!
OK.
RATTLESNAKE VALLEY
TELEGRAPH
HEY, TOM, MESSAGE FOR YOU... URGENT, APPARENTLY.
I RIDE AN OLD PAINT...
MEANWHILE, THE FUGITIVE IS STILL RIDING...
WATER, AT LAST! JUST IN TIME...
POISONOUS WATER
One drink and you'll NEVER be thirsty again
IT'S SO HOT! UNLESS I FIND SOME WATER SOON, OUR BONES WILL BE BLEACHED BY THE SUN...
SAY...
DANGER NON-DRINKABLE WATER
Arrange your affairs before drinking
MORRIS
LKALINE WATER
ON-DRINKABLE!
For all your funerary needs, speak to TOM O'SULLIVAN (Founded 1809)
139

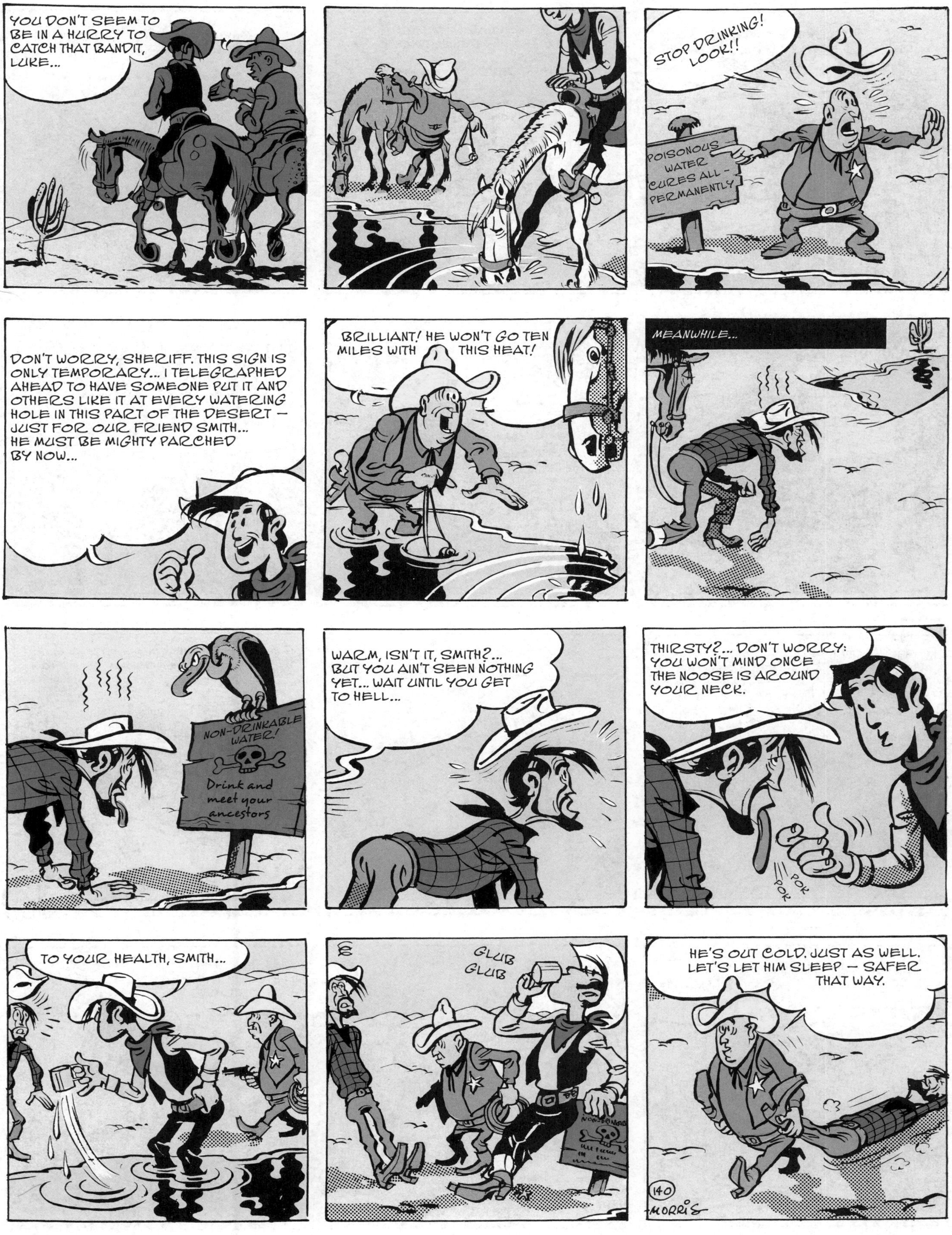

YOU DON'T SEEM TO BE IN A HURRY TO CATCH THAT BANDIT, LUKE...
STOP DRINKING! LOOK!!
POISONOUS WATER CURES ALL - PERMANENTLY
DON'T WORRY, SHERIFF. THIS SIGN IS ONLY TEMPORARY... I TELEGRAPHED AHEAD TO HAVE SOMEONE PUT IT AND OTHERS LIKE IT AT EVERY WATERING HOLE IN THIS PART OF THE DESERT - JUST FOR OUR FRIEND SMITH... HE MUST BE MIGHTY PARCHED BY NOW...
BRILLIANT! HE WON'T GO TEN MILES WITH THIS HEAT!
MEANWHILE...
NON-DRINKABLE WATER!
Drink and meet your ancestors
WARM, ISN'T IT, SMITH?... BUT YOU AIN'T SEEN NOTHING YET... WAIT UNTIL YOU GET TO HELL...
THIRSTY?... DON'T WORRY: YOU WON'T MIND ONCE THE NOOSE IS AROUND YOUR NECK.
POK
POK
TO YOUR HEALTH, SMITH...
GLUB GLUB
HE'S OUT COLD. JUST AS WELL. LET'S LET HIM SLEEP - SAFER THAT WAY.
140
MORRIS

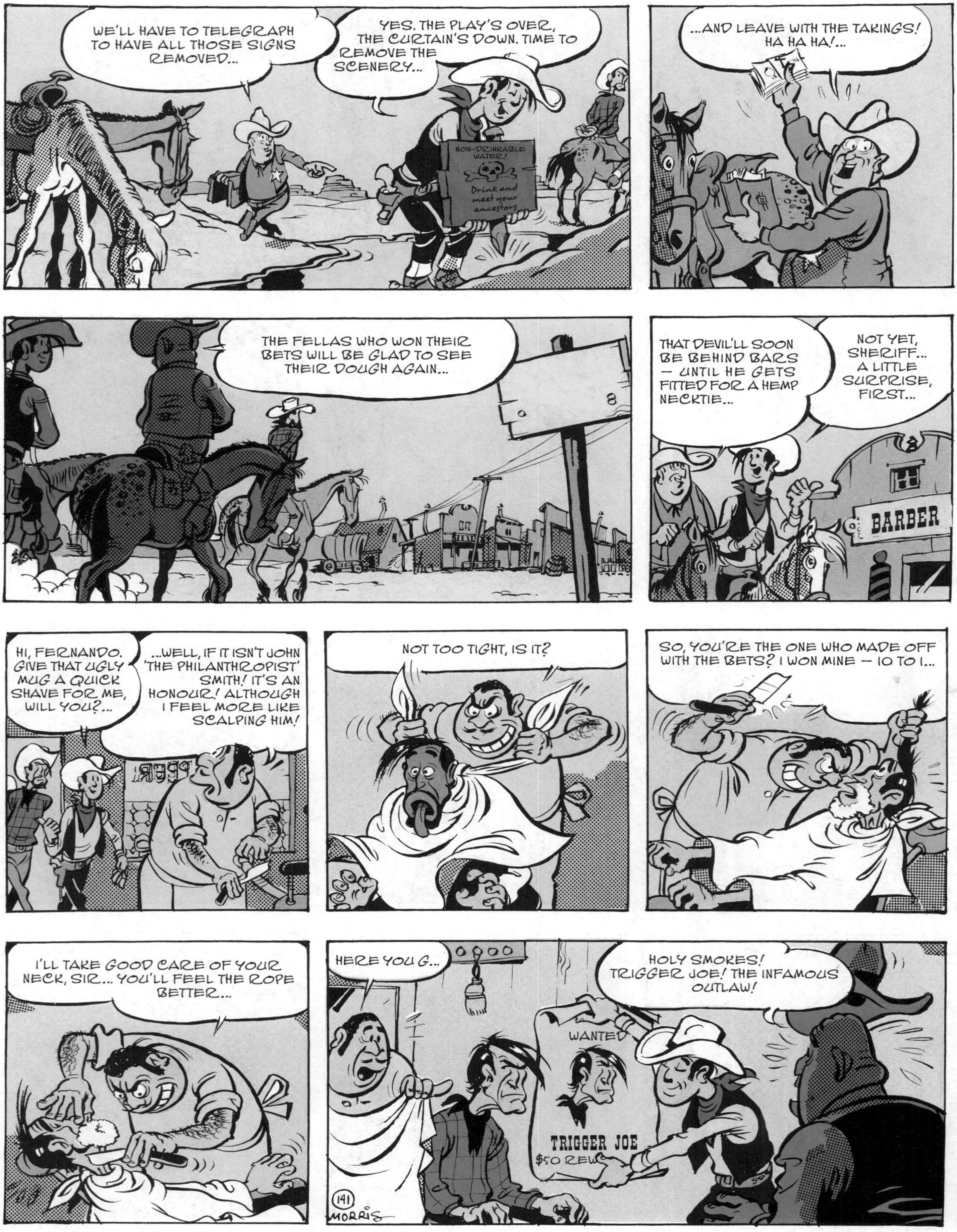
WE'LL HAVE TO TELEGRAPH TO HAVE ALL THOSE SIGNS REMOVED...
YES. THE PLAY'S OVER, THE CURTAIN'S DOWN. TIME TO REMOVE THE SCENERY...
NON-DRINKABLE WATER! Drink and meet your ancestors
...AND LEAVE WITH THE TAKINGS! HA HA HA!...
THE FELLAS WHO WON THEIR BETS WILL BE GLAD TO SEE THEIR DOUGH AGAIN...
THAT DEVIL'LL SOON BE BEHIND BARS — UNTIL HE GETS FITTED FOR A HEMP NECKTIE...
NOT YET, SHERIFF... A LITTLE SURPRISE, FIRST...
BARBER
HI, FERNANDO. GIVE THAT UGLY MUG A QUICK SHAVE FOR ME, WILL YOU?...
...WELL, IF IT ISN'T JOHN 'THE PHILANTHROPIST' SMITH! IT'S AN HONOUR! ALTHOUGH I FEEL MORE LIKE SCALPING HIM!
NOT TOO TIGHT, IS IT?
SO, YOU'RE THE ONE WHO MADE OFF WITH THE BETS? I WON MINE — 10 TO 1...
I'LL TAKE GOOD CARE OF YOUR NECK, SIR... YOU'LL FEEL THE ROPE BETTER...
HERE YOU G...
HOLY SMOKES! TRIGGER JOE! THE INFAMOUS OUTLAW!
WANTED
TRIGGER JOE
$50 REW
141
MORRIS

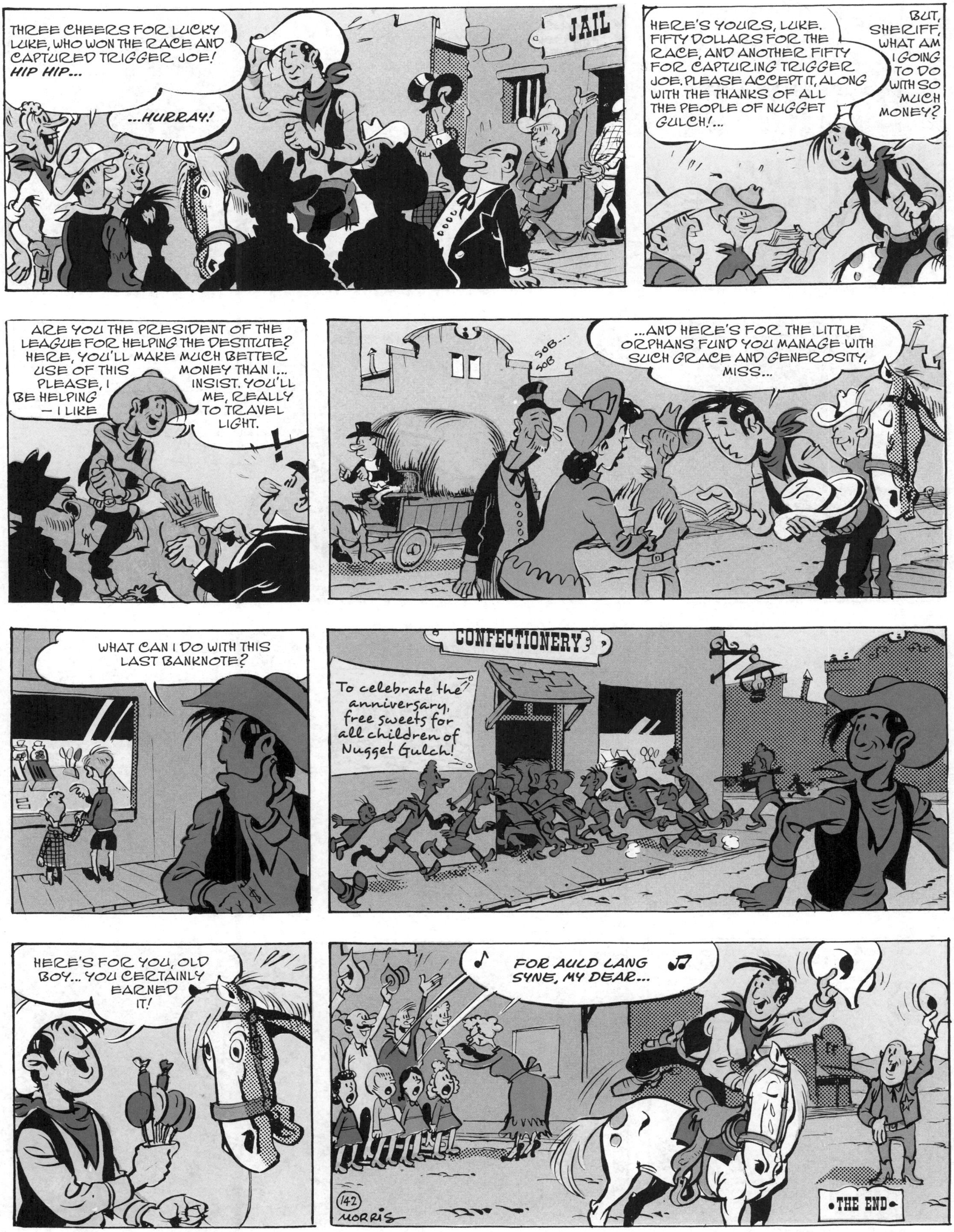
THREE CHEERS FOR LUCKY LUKE, WHO WON THE RACE AND CAPTURED TRIGGER JOE! HIP HIP...
...HURRAY!
JAIL
HERE'S YOURS, LUKE. FIFTY DOLLARS FOR THE RACE, AND ANOTHER FIFTY FOR CAPTURING TRIGGER JOE. PLEASE ACCEPT IT, ALONG WITH THE THANKS OF ALL THE PEOPLE OF NUGGET GULCH!...
BUT, SHERIFF, WHAT AM I GOING TO DO WITH SO MUCH MONEY?
ARE YOU THE PRESIDENT OF THE LEAGUE FOR HELPING THE DESTITUTE? HERE, YOU'LL MAKE MUCH BETTER USE OF THIS MONEY THAN I... PLEASE, I INSIST. YOU'LL BE HELPING ME, REALLY — I LIKE TO TRAVEL LIGHT.
SOB... SOB
...AND HERE'S FOR THE LITTLE ORPHANS FUND YOU MANAGE WITH SUCH GRACE AND GENEROSITY, MISS...
WHAT CAN I DO WITH THIS LAST BANKNOTE?
CONFECTIONERY
To celebrate the anniversary, free sweets for all children of Nugget Gulch!
HERE'S FOR YOU, OLD BOY... YOU CERTAINLY EARNED IT!
FOR AULD LANG SYNE, MY DEAR...
142
MORRIS
THE END

ROUND-UP DAYS

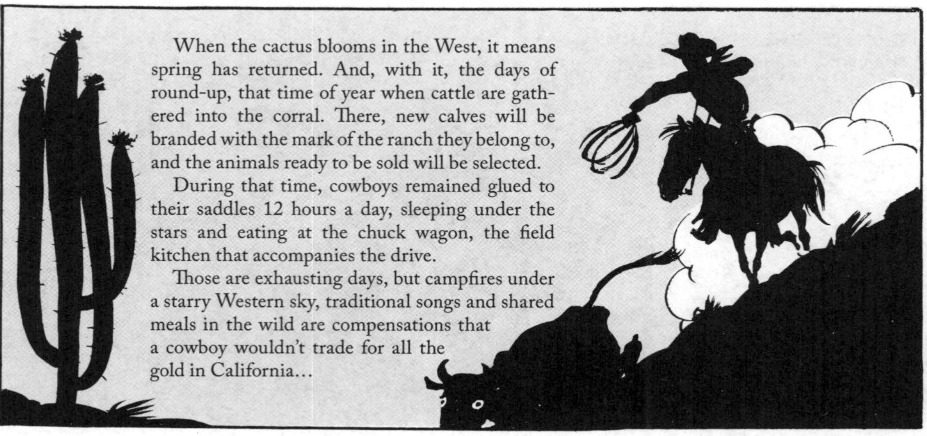

When the cactus blooms in the West, it means spring has returned. And, with it, the days of round-up, that time of year when cattle are gathered into the corral. There, new calves will be branded with the mark of the ranch they belong to, and the animals ready to be sold will be selected.

During that time, cowboys remained glued to their saddles 12 hours a day, sleeping under the stars and eating at the chuck wagon, the field kitchen that accompanies the drive.

Those are exhausting days, but campfires under a starry Western sky, traditional songs and shared meals in the wild are compensations that a cowboy wouldn't trade for all the gold in California…

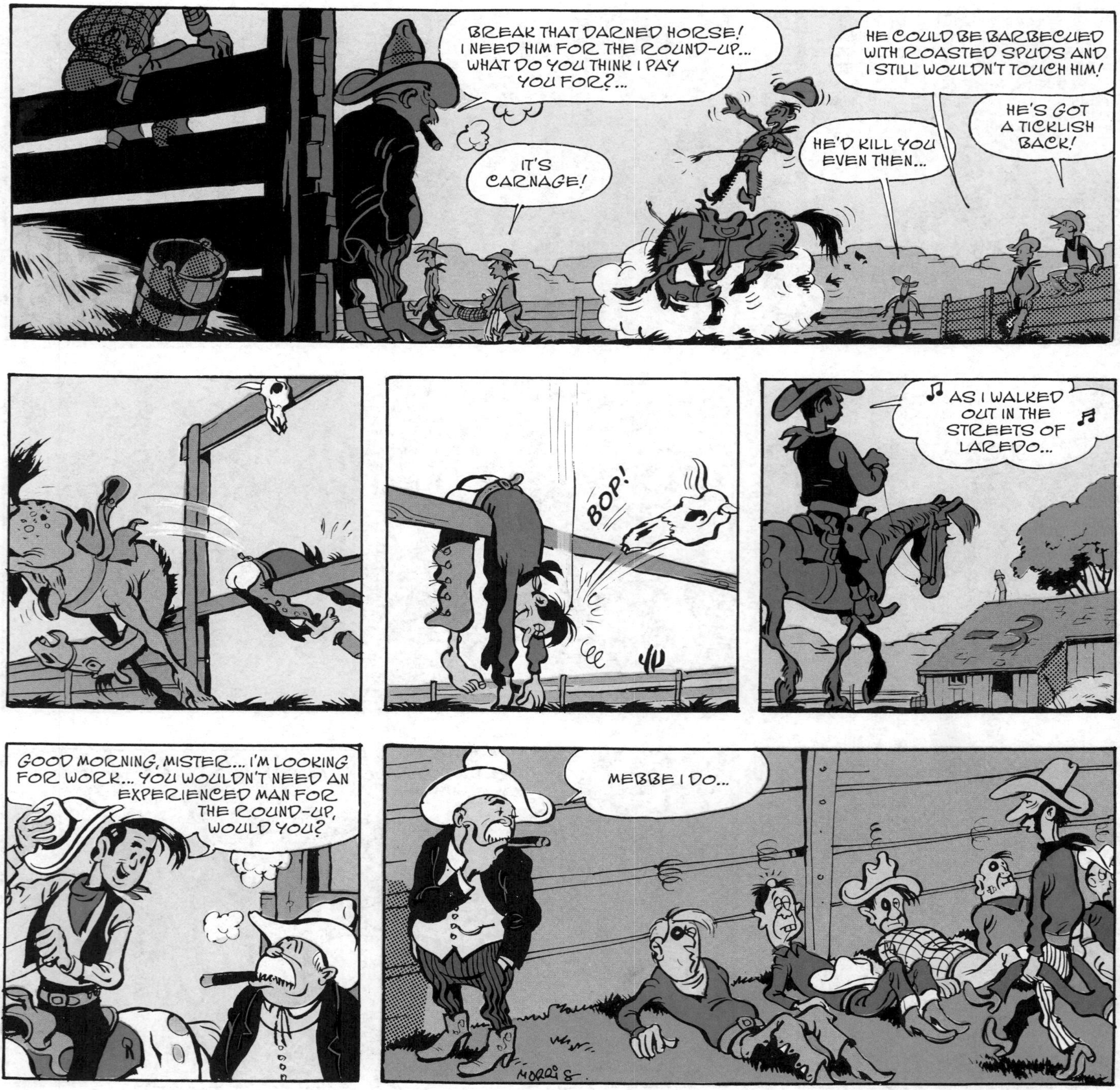
BREAK THAT DARNED HORSE! I NEED HIM FOR THE ROUND-UP... WHAT DO YOU THINK I PAY YOU FOR?...
IT'S CARNAGE!
HE COULD BE BARBECUED WITH ROASTED SPUDS AND I STILL WOULDN'T TOUCH HIM!
HE'D KILL YOU EVEN THEN...
HE'S GOT A TICKLISH BACK!
BOP!
AS I WALKED OUT IN THE STREETS OF LAREDO...
GOOD MORNING, MISTER... I'M LOOKING FOR WORK... YOU WOULDN'T NEED AN EXPERIENCED MAN FOR THE ROUND-UP, WOULD YOU?
MEBBE I DO...
MORRIS

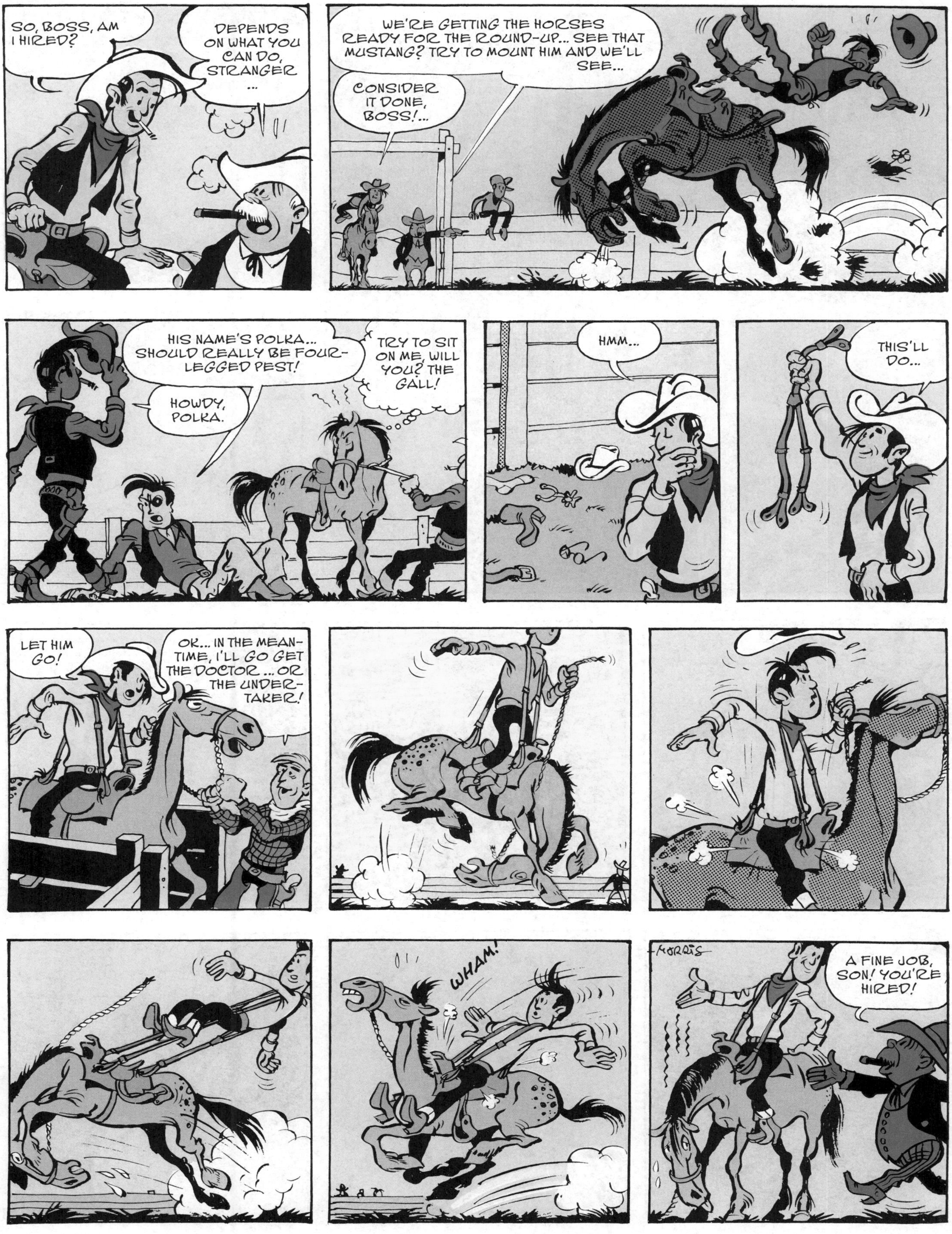
SO, BOSS, AM I HIRED?
DEPENDS ON WHAT YOU CAN DO, STRANGER ...
WE'RE GETTING THE HORSES READY FOR THE ROUND-UP... SEE THAT MUSTANG? TRY TO MOUNT HIM AND WE'LL SEE...
CONSIDER IT DONE, BOSS!...
HIS NAME'S POLKA... SHOULD REALLY BE FOUR-LEGGED PEST!
HOWDY, POLKA.
TRY TO SIT ON ME, WILL YOU? THE GALL!
HMM...
THIS'LL DO...
LET HIM GO!
OK... IN THE MEAN-TIME, I'LL GO GET THE DOCTOR ...OR THE UNDER-TAKER!
WHAM!
MORRIS
A FINE JOB, SON! YOU'RE HIRED!

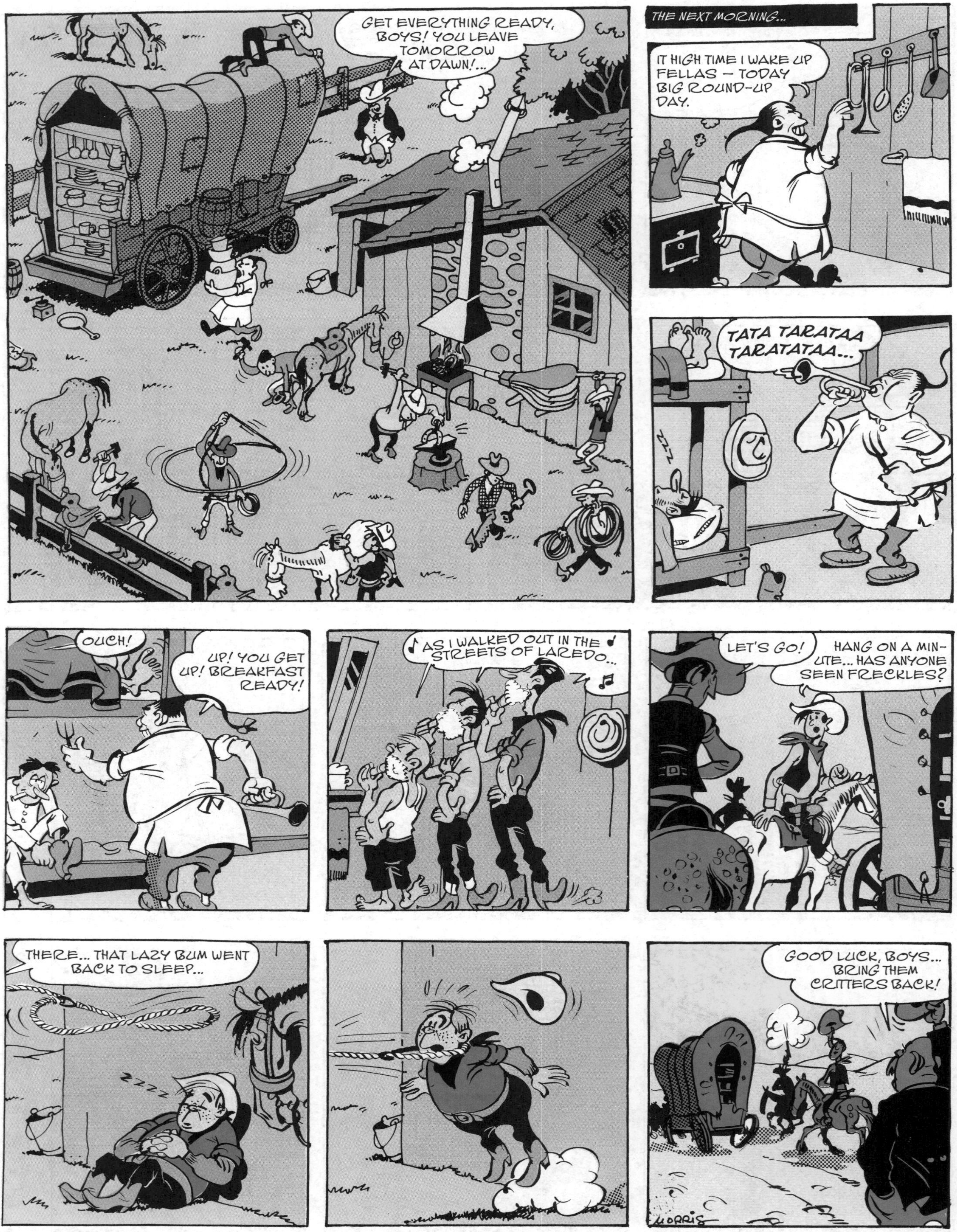
GET EVERYTHING READY, BOYS! YOU LEAVE TOMORROW AT DAWN!...
THE NEXT MORNING...
IT HIGH TIME I WAKE UP FELLAS — TODAY BIG ROUND-UP DAY.
TATA TARATAA TARATATAA...
OUCH!
UP! YOU GET UP! BREAKFAST READY!
AS I WALKED OUT IN THE STREETS OF LAREDO...
LET'S GO!
HANG ON A MINUTE... HAS ANYONE SEEN FRECKLES?
THERE... THAT LAZY BUM WENT BACK TO SLEEP...
ZZZZ
GOOD LUCK, BOYS... BRING THEM CRITTERS BACK!
MORRIS

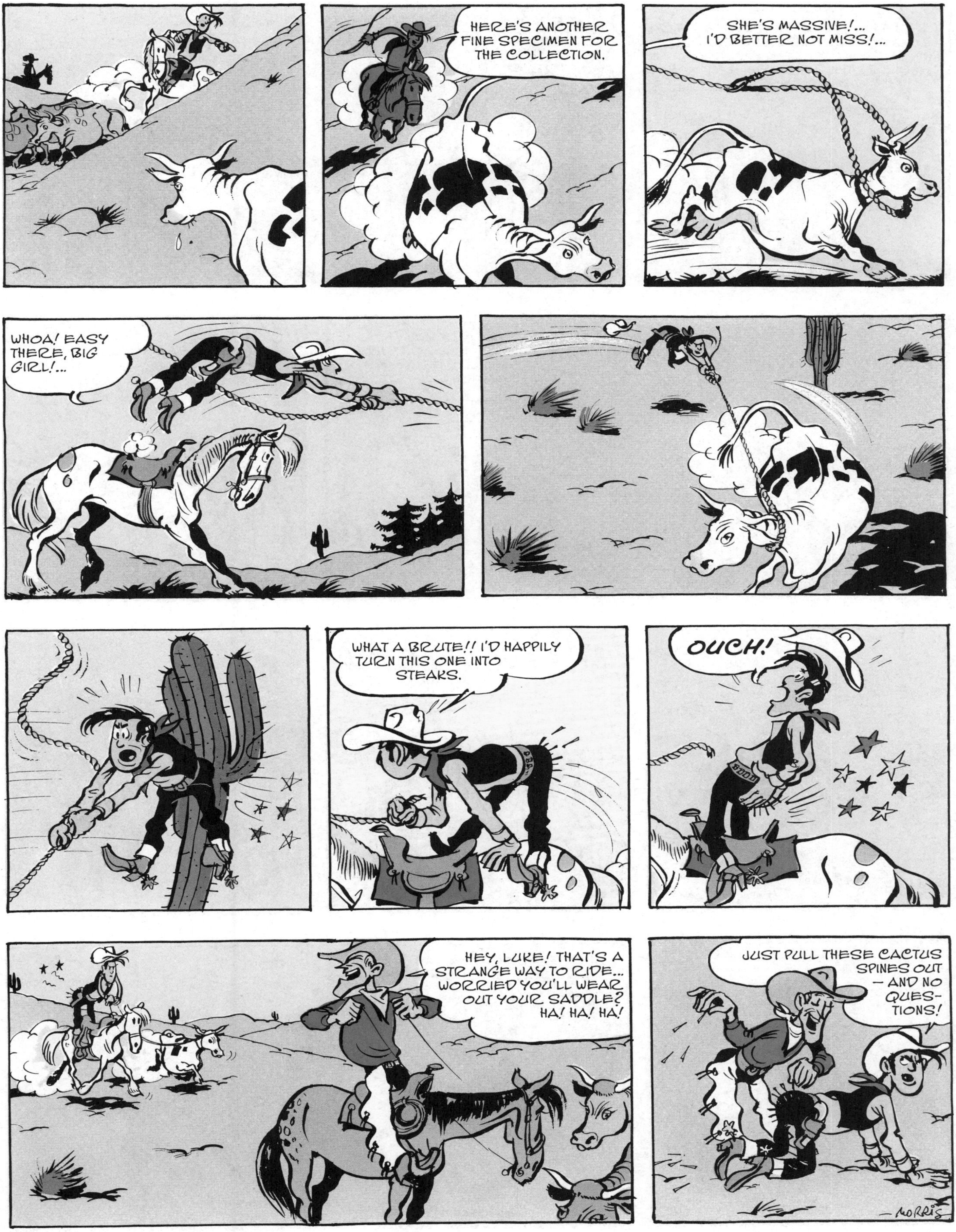
HERE'S ANOTHER FINE SPECIMEN FOR THE COLLECTION.
SHE'S MASSIVE!... I'D BETTER NOT MISS!...
WHOA! EASY THERE, BIG GIRL!...
WHAT A BRUTE!! I'D HAPPILY TURN THIS ONE INTO STEAKS.
OUCH!
HEY, LUKE! THAT'S A STRANGE WAY TO RIDE... WORRIED YOU'LL WEAR OUT YOUR SADDLE? HA! HA! HA!
JUST PULL THESE CACTUS SPINES OUT – AND NO QUES-TIONS!
MORRIS

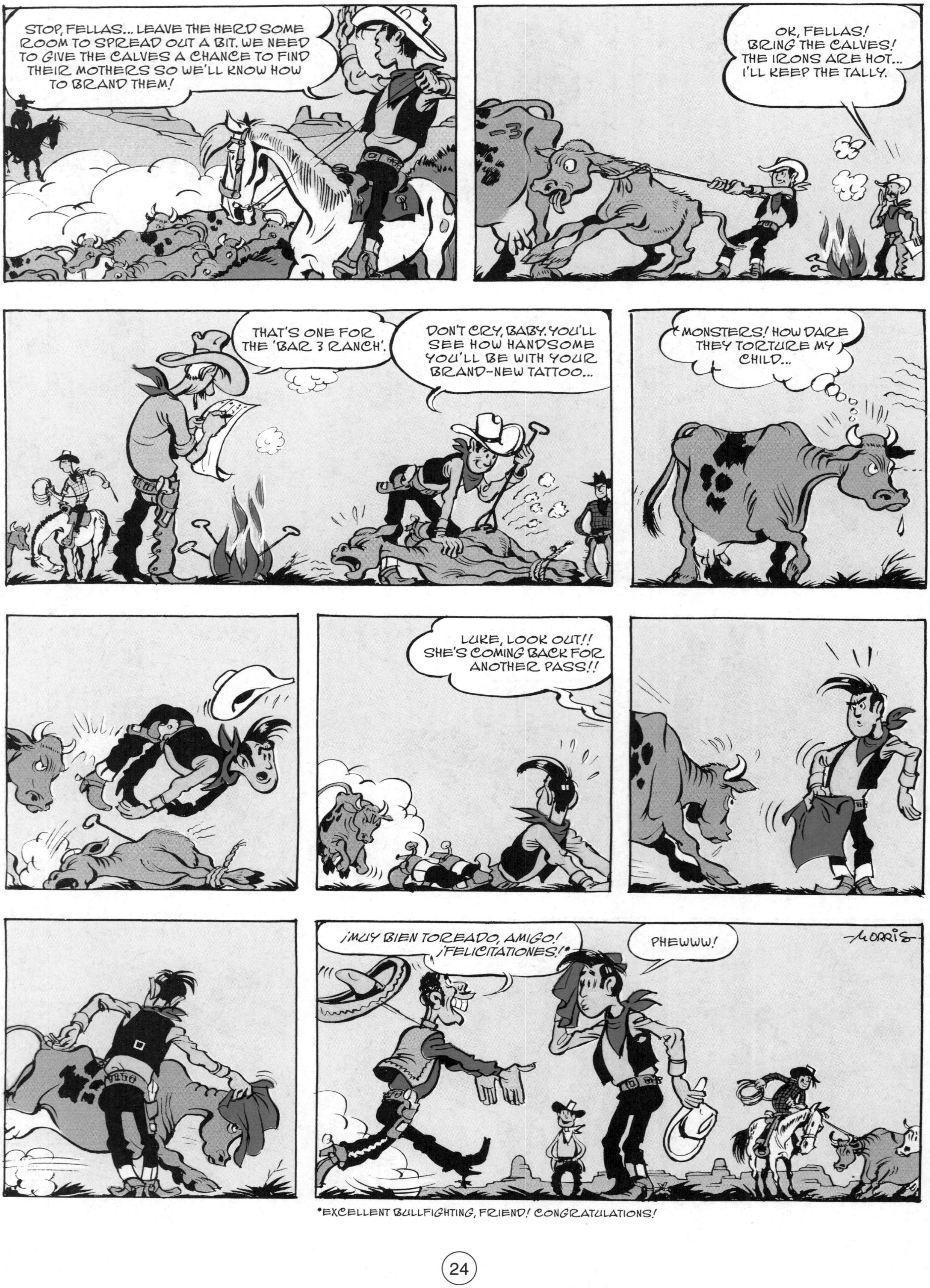
STOP, FELLAS... LEAVE THE HERD SOME ROOM TO SPREAD OUT A BIT. WE NEED TO GIVE THE CALVES A CHANCE TO FIND THEIR MOTHERS SO WE'LL KNOW HOW TO BRAND THEM!
OK, FELLAS! BRING THE CALVES! THE IRONS ARE HOT... I'LL KEEP THE TALLY.
THAT'S ONE FOR THE 'BAR 3 RANCH'.
DON'T CRY, BABY. YOU'LL SEE HOW HANDSOME YOU'LL BE WITH YOUR BRAND-NEW TATTOO...
MONSTERS! HOW DARE THEY TORTURE MY CHILD...
LUKE, LOOK OUT!! SHE'S COMING BACK FOR ANOTHER PASS!!
¡MUY BIEN TOREADO, AMIGO! ¡FELICITATIONES!*
PHEWWW!
MORRIS

*EXCELLENT BULLFIGHTING, FRIEND! CONGRATULATIONS!

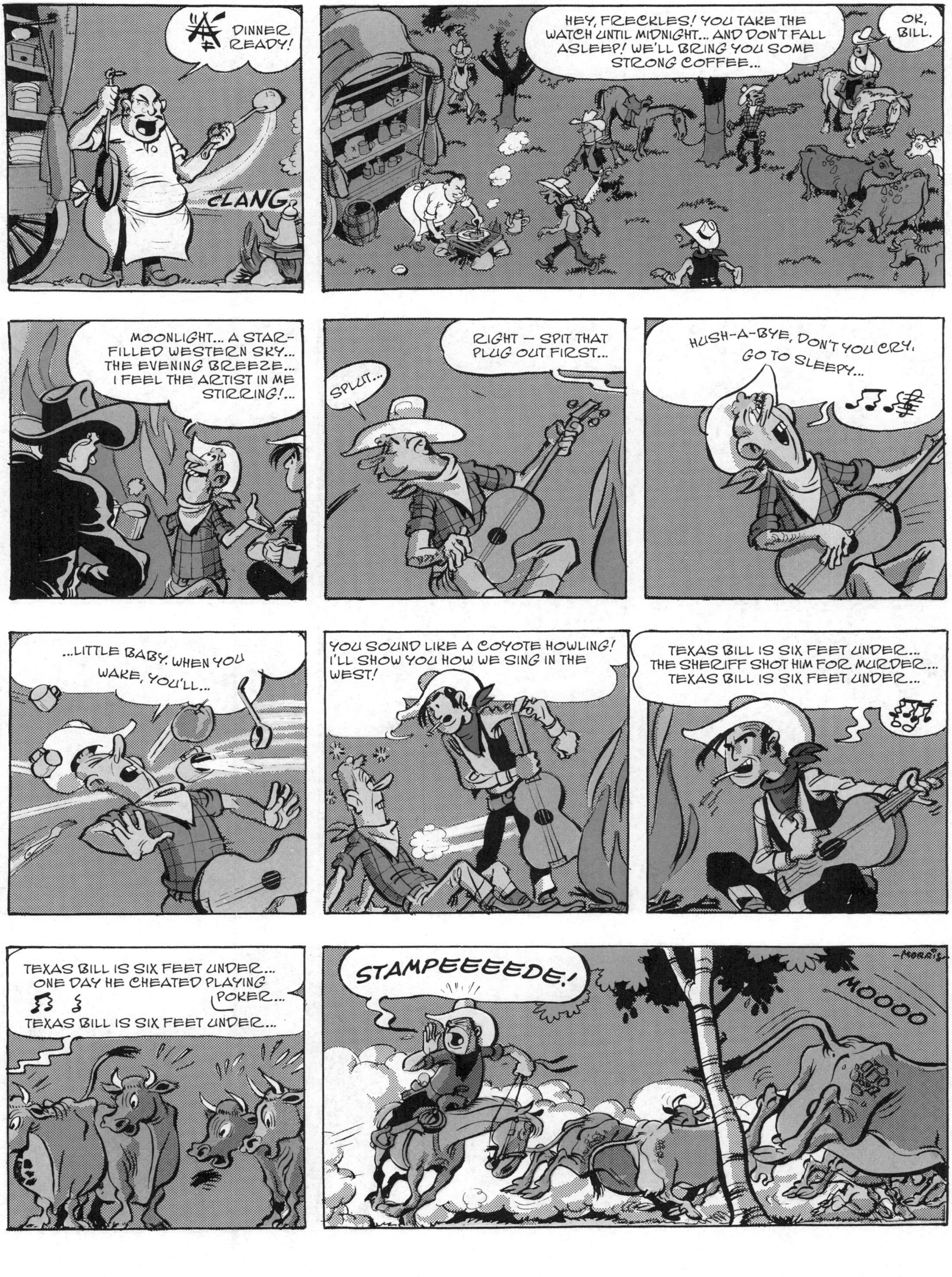
DINNER READY!
CLANG
HEY, FRECKLES! YOU TAKE THE WATCH UNTIL MIDNIGHT... AND DON'T FALL ASLEEP! WE'LL BRING YOU SOME STRONG COFFEE...
OK, BILL.
MOONLIGHT... A STAR-FILLED WESTERN SKY... THE EVENING BREEZE... I FEEL THE ARTIST IN ME STIRRING!...
RIGHT — SPIT THAT PLUG OUT FIRST...
SPLUT...
HUSH-A-BYE, DON'T YOU CRY, GO TO SLEEPY...
...LITTLE BABY. WHEN YOU WAKE, YOU'LL...
YOU SOUND LIKE A COYOTE HOWLING! I'LL SHOW YOU HOW WE SING IN THE WEST!
TEXAS BILL IS SIX FEET UNDER... THE SHERIFF SHOT HIM FOR MURDER... TEXAS BILL IS SIX FEET UNDER...
TEXAS BILL IS SIX FEET UNDER... ONE DAY HE CHEATED PLAYING POKER... TEXAS BILL IS SIX FEET UNDER...
STAMPEEEEEDE!
MOOOO
MORRIS

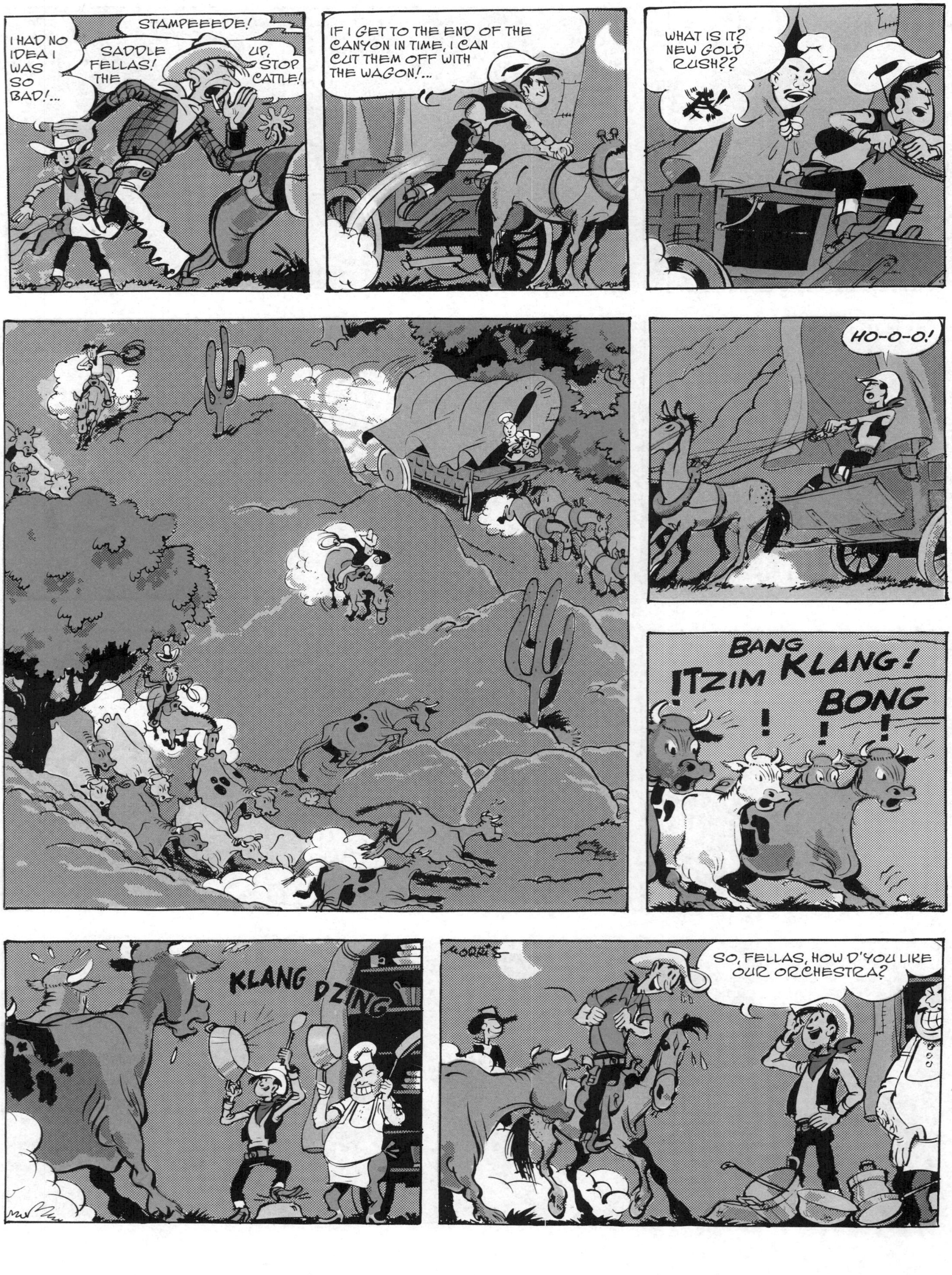
STAMPEEEDE!
SADDLE FELLAS! THE
UP, STOP CATTLE!
I HAD NO IDEA I WAS SO BAD!...
IF I GET TO THE END OF THE CANYON IN TIME, I CAN CUT THEM OFF WITH THE WAGON!...
WHAT IS IT? NEW GOLD RUSH??
HO-O-O!
BANG
KLANG!
ITZIM
BONG
KLANG
DZING
SO, FELLAS, HOW D'YOU LIKE OUR ORCHESTRA?

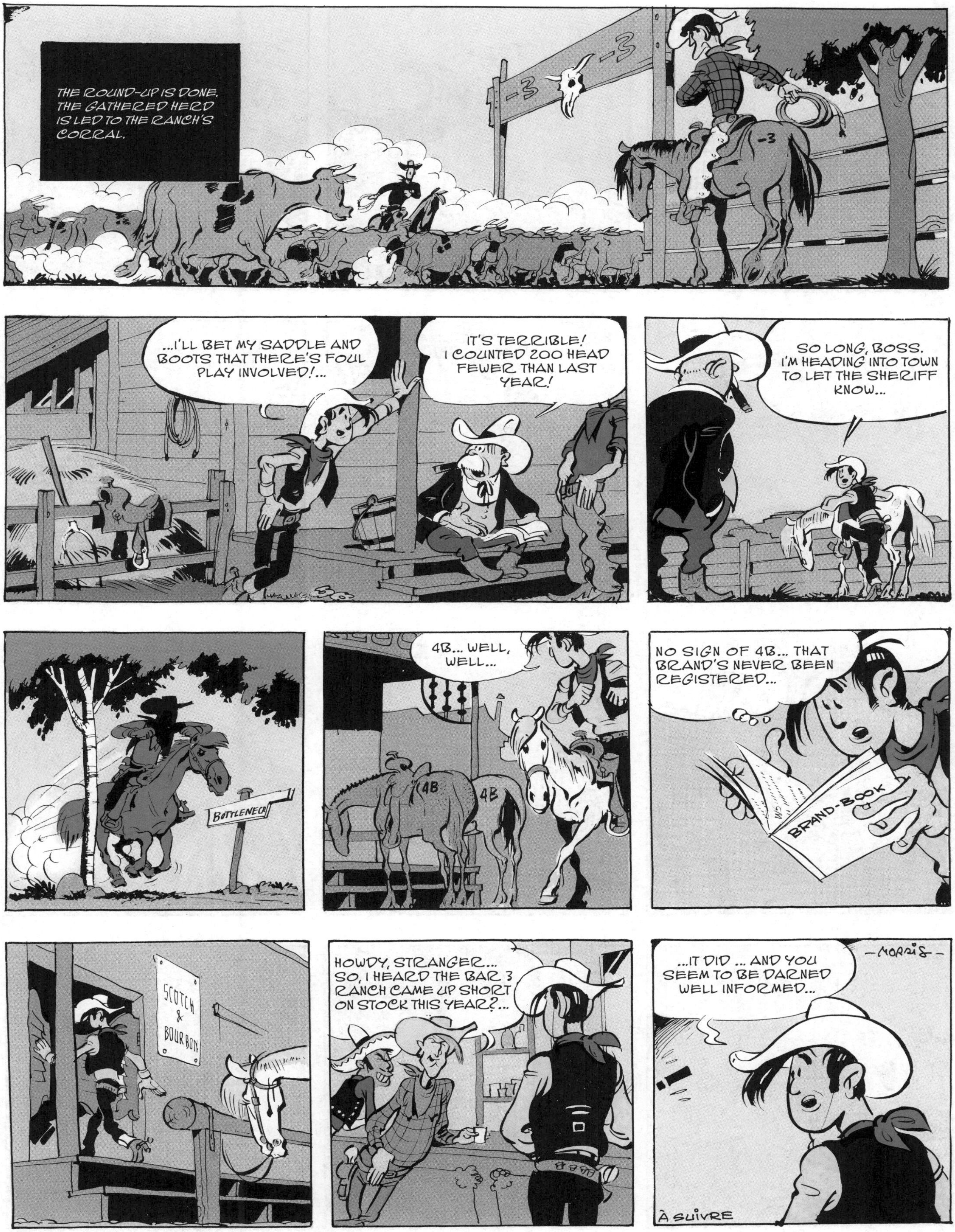
THE ROUND-UP IS DONE. THE GATHERED HERD IS LED TO THE RANCH'S CORRAL.
...I'LL BET MY SADDLE AND BOOTS THAT THERE'S FOUL PLAY INVOLVED!...
IT'S TERRIBLE! I COUNTED 200 HEAD FEWER THAN LAST YEAR!
SO LONG, BOSS. I'M HEADING INTO TOWN TO LET THE SHERIFF KNOW...
BOTTLENECK
4B... WELL, WELL...
4B
4B
NO SIGN OF 4B... THAT BRAND'S NEVER BEEN REGISTERED...
BRAND-BOOK
SCOTCH & BOURBON
HOWDY, STRANGER... SO, I HEARD THE BAR 3 RANCH CAME UP SHORT ON STOCK THIS YEAR?...
...IT DID ... AND YOU SEEM TO BE DARNED WELL INFORMED...
-MORRIS-
À SUIVRE

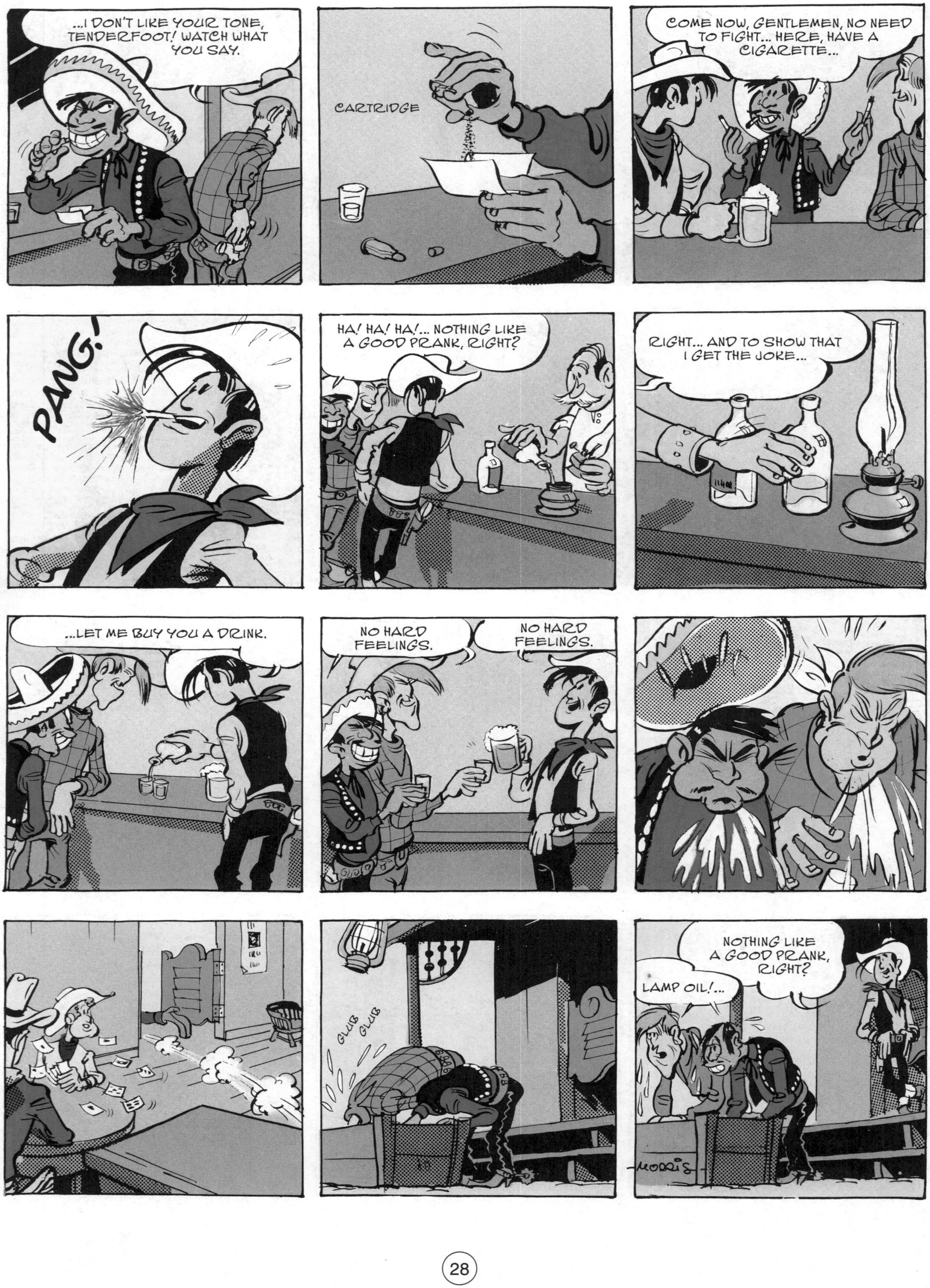

...I DON'T LIKE YOUR TONE, TENDERFOOT! WATCH WHAT YOU SAY.
CARTRIDGE
COME NOW, GENTLEMEN, NO NEED TO FIGHT... HERE, HAVE A CIGARETTE...
PANG!
HA! HA! HA!... NOTHING LIKE A GOOD PRANK, RIGHT?
RIGHT... AND TO SHOW THAT I GET THE JOKE...
...LET ME BUY YOU A DRINK.
NO HARD FEELINGS.
NO HARD FEELINGS.
GLUB GLUB
LAMP OIL!...
NOTHING LIKE A GOOD PRANK, RIGHT?
MORRIS

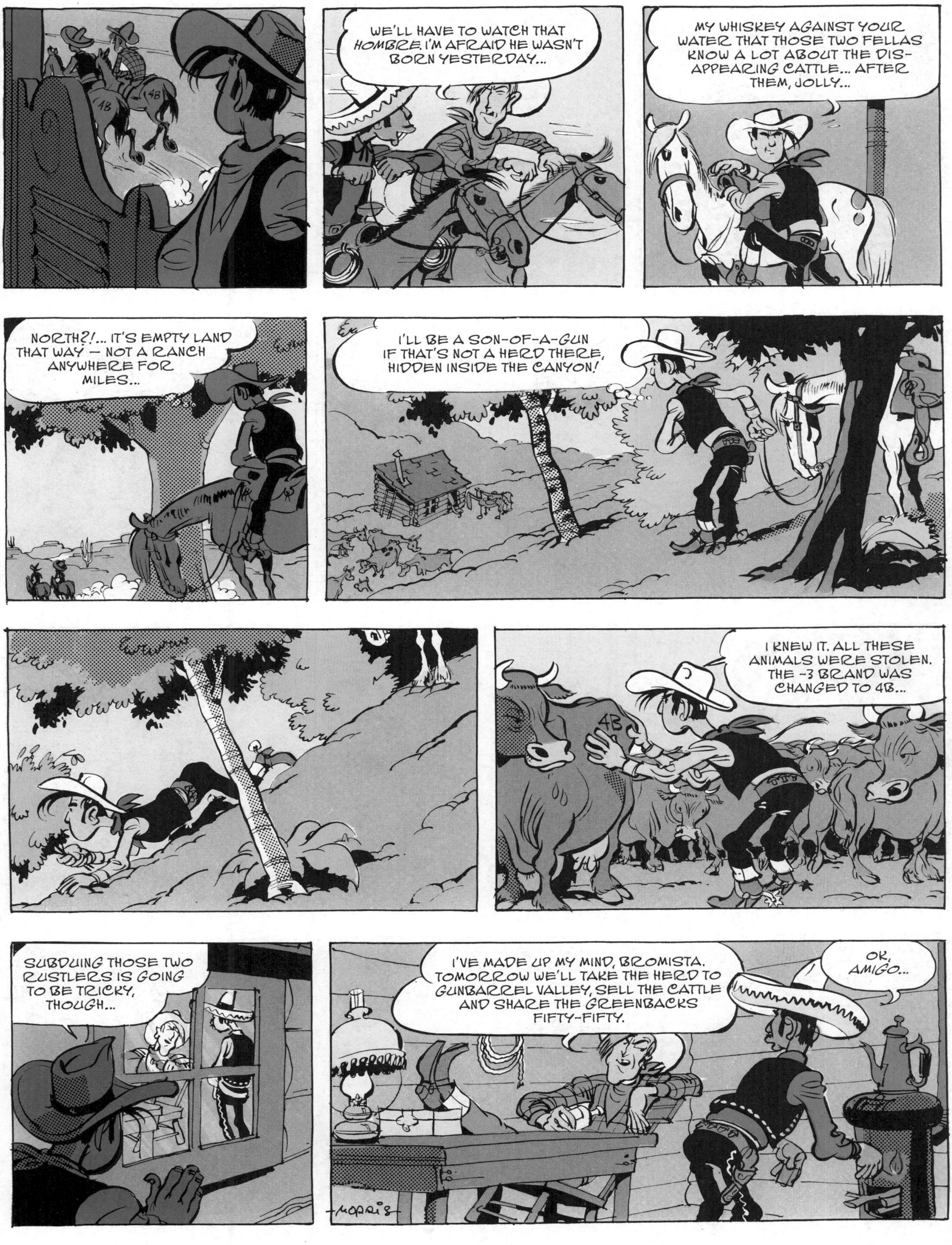
WE'LL HAVE TO WATCH THAT HOMBRE. I'M AFRAID HE WASN'T BORN YESTERDAY...
MY WHISKEY AGAINST YOUR WATER THAT THOSE TWO FELLAS KNOW A LOT ABOUT THE DIS-APPEARING CATTLE... AFTER THEM, JOLLY...
NORTH?!... IT'S EMPTY LAND THAT WAY — NOT A RANCH ANYWHERE FOR MILES...
I'LL BE A SON-OF-A-GUN IF THAT'S NOT A HERD THERE, HIDDEN INSIDE THE CANYON!
I KNEW IT. ALL THESE ANIMALS WERE STOLEN. THE -3 BRAND WAS CHANGED TO 4B...
SUBDUING THOSE TWO RUSTLERS IS GOING TO BE TRICKY, THOUGH...
I'VE MADE UP MY MIND, BROMISTA. TOMORROW WE'LL TAKE THE HERD TO GUNBARREL VALLEY, SELL THE CATTLE AND SHARE THE GREENBACKS FIFTY-FIFTY.
OK, AMIGO...
MORRIS

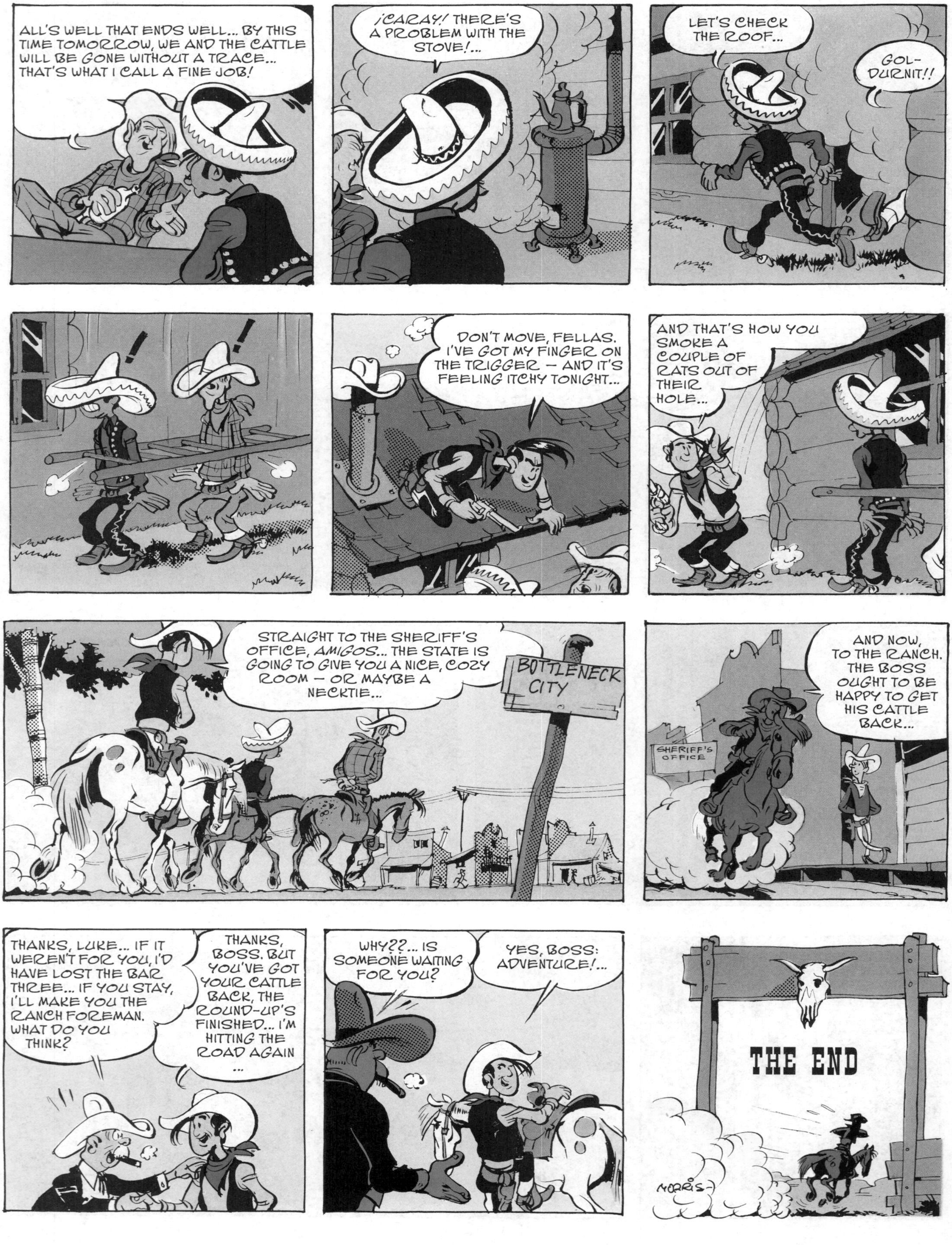

ALL'S WELL THAT ENDS WELL... BY THIS TIME TOMORROW, WE AND THE CATTLE WILL BE GONE WITHOUT A TRACE... THAT'S WHAT I CALL A FINE JOB!
¡CARAY! THERE'S A PROBLEM WITH THE STOVE!...
LET'S CHECK THE ROOF...
GOL-DURNIT!!
DON'T MOVE, FELLAS. I'VE GOT MY FINGER ON THE TRIGGER — AND IT'S FEELING ITCHY TONIGHT...
AND THAT'S HOW YOU SMOKE A COUPLE OF RATS OUT OF THEIR HOLE...
STRAIGHT TO THE SHERIFF'S OFFICE, AMIGOS... THE STATE IS GOING TO GIVE YOU A NICE, COZY ROOM — OR MAYBE A NECKTIE...
BOTTLENECK CITY
AND NOW, TO THE RANCH. THE BOSS OUGHT TO BE HAPPY TO GET HIS CATTLE BACK...
SHERIFF'S OFFICE
THANKS, LUKE... IF IT WEREN'T FOR YOU, I'D HAVE LOST THE BAR THREE... IF YOU STAY, I'LL MAKE YOU THE RANCH FOREMAN. WHAT DO YOU THINK?
THANKS, BOSS. BUT YOU'VE GOT YOUR CATTLE BACK, THE ROUND-UP'S FINISHED... I'M HITTING THE ROAD AGAIN ...
WHY??... IS SOMEONE WAITING FOR YOU?
YES, BOSS: ADVENTURE!...
THE END
MORRIS

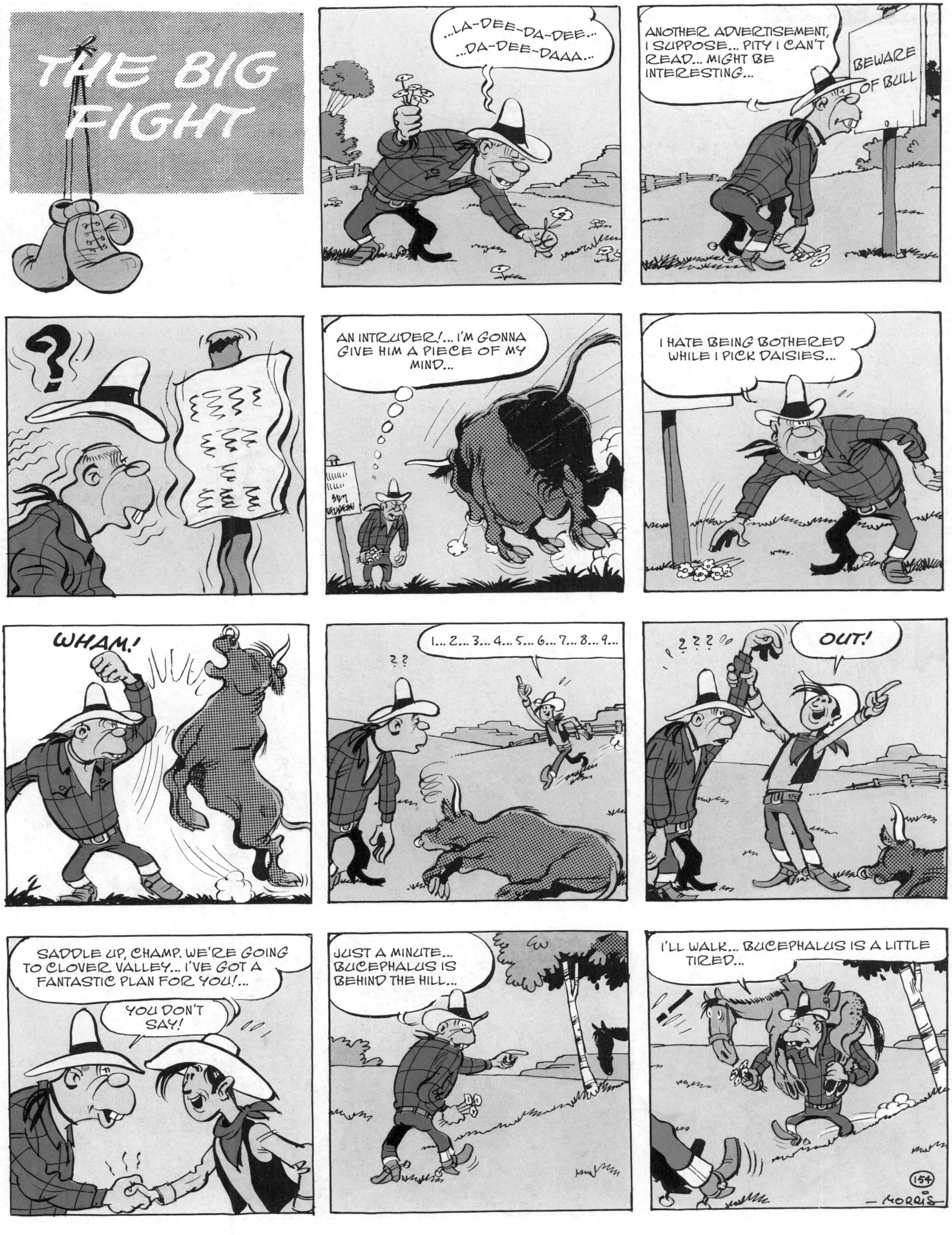
THE BIG FIGHT
...LA-DEE-DA-DEE... ...DA-DEE-DAAA...
ANOTHER ADVERTISEMENT, I SUPPOSE... PITY I CAN'T READ... MIGHT BE INTERESTING...
BEWARE OF BULL
?
AN INTRUDER!... I'M GONNA GIVE HIM A PIECE OF MY MIND...
I HATE BEING BOTHERED WHILE I PICK DAISIES...
WHAM!
? ?
1... 2... 3... 4... 5... 6... 7... 8... 9...
? ? ?
OUT!
SADDLE UP, CHAMP. WE'RE GOING TO CLOVER VALLEY... I'VE GOT A FANTASTIC PLAN FOR YOU!...
YOU DON'T SAY!
JUST A MINUTE... BUCEPHALUS IS BEHIND THE HILL...
I'LL WALK... BUCEPHALUS IS A LITTLE TIRED...
!
154
MORRIS

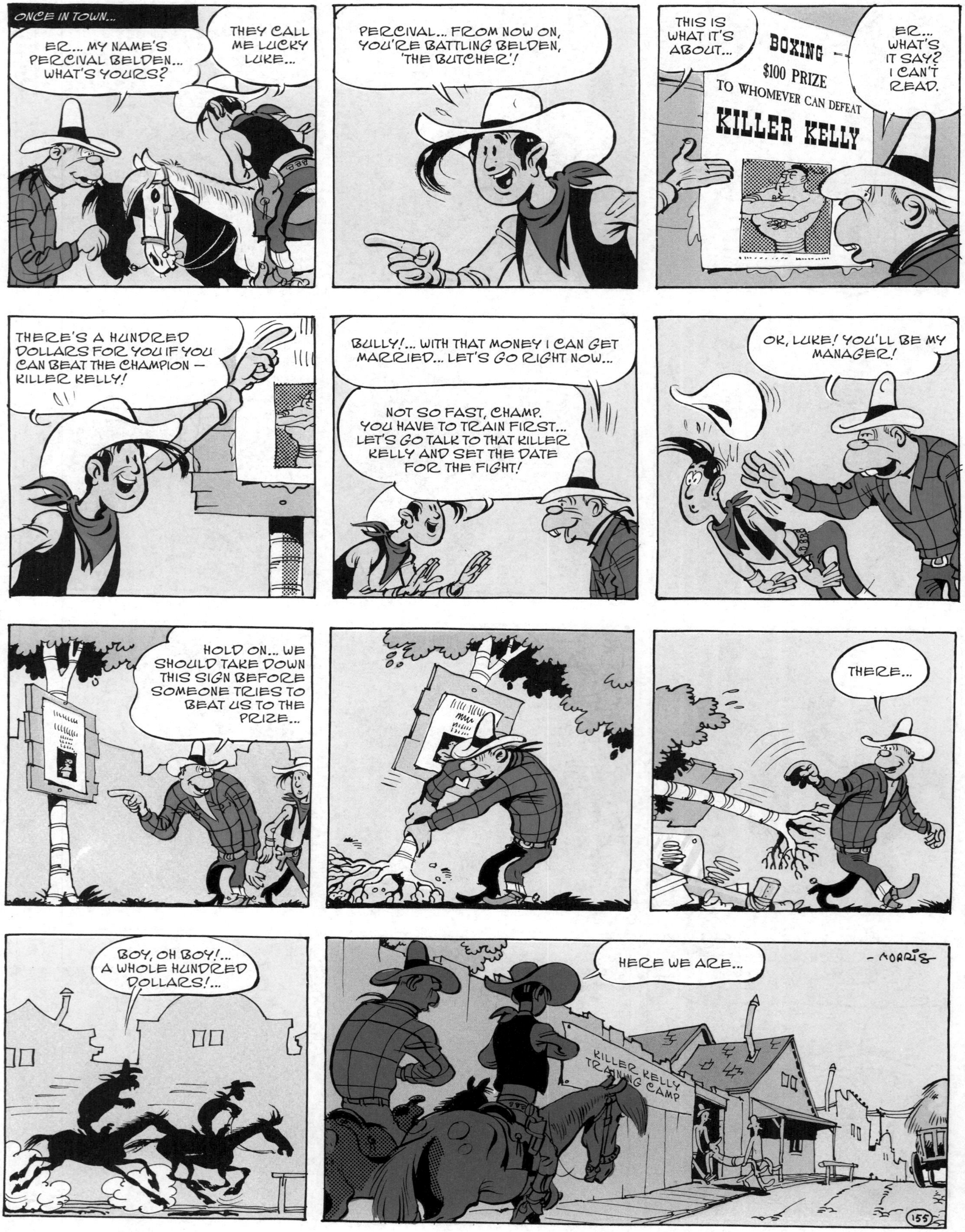
ONCE IN TOWN...
ER... MY NAME'S PERCIVAL BELDEN... WHAT'S YOURS?
THEY CALL ME LUCKY LUKE...
PERCIVAL... FROM NOW ON, YOU'RE BATTLING BELDEN, 'THE BUTCHER'!
THIS IS WHAT IT'S ABOUT...
BOXING
$100 PRIZE
TO WHOMEVER CAN DEFEAT
KILLER KELLY
ER... WHAT'S IT SAY? I CAN'T READ.
THERE'S A HUNDRED DOLLARS FOR YOU IF YOU CAN BEAT THE CHAMPION — KILLER KELLY!
BULLY!... WITH THAT MONEY I CAN GET MARRIED... LET'S GO RIGHT NOW...
NOT SO FAST, CHAMP. YOU HAVE TO TRAIN FIRST... LET'S GO TALK TO THAT KILLER KELLY AND SET THE DATE FOR THE FIGHT!
OK, LUKE! YOU'LL BE MY MANAGER!
HOLD ON... WE SHOULD TAKE DOWN THIS SIGN BEFORE SOMEONE TRIES TO BEAT US TO THE PRIZE...
THERE...
BOY, OH BOY!... A WHOLE HUNDRED DOLLARS!...
HERE WE ARE...
KILLER KELLY TRAINING CAMP
MORRIS
155

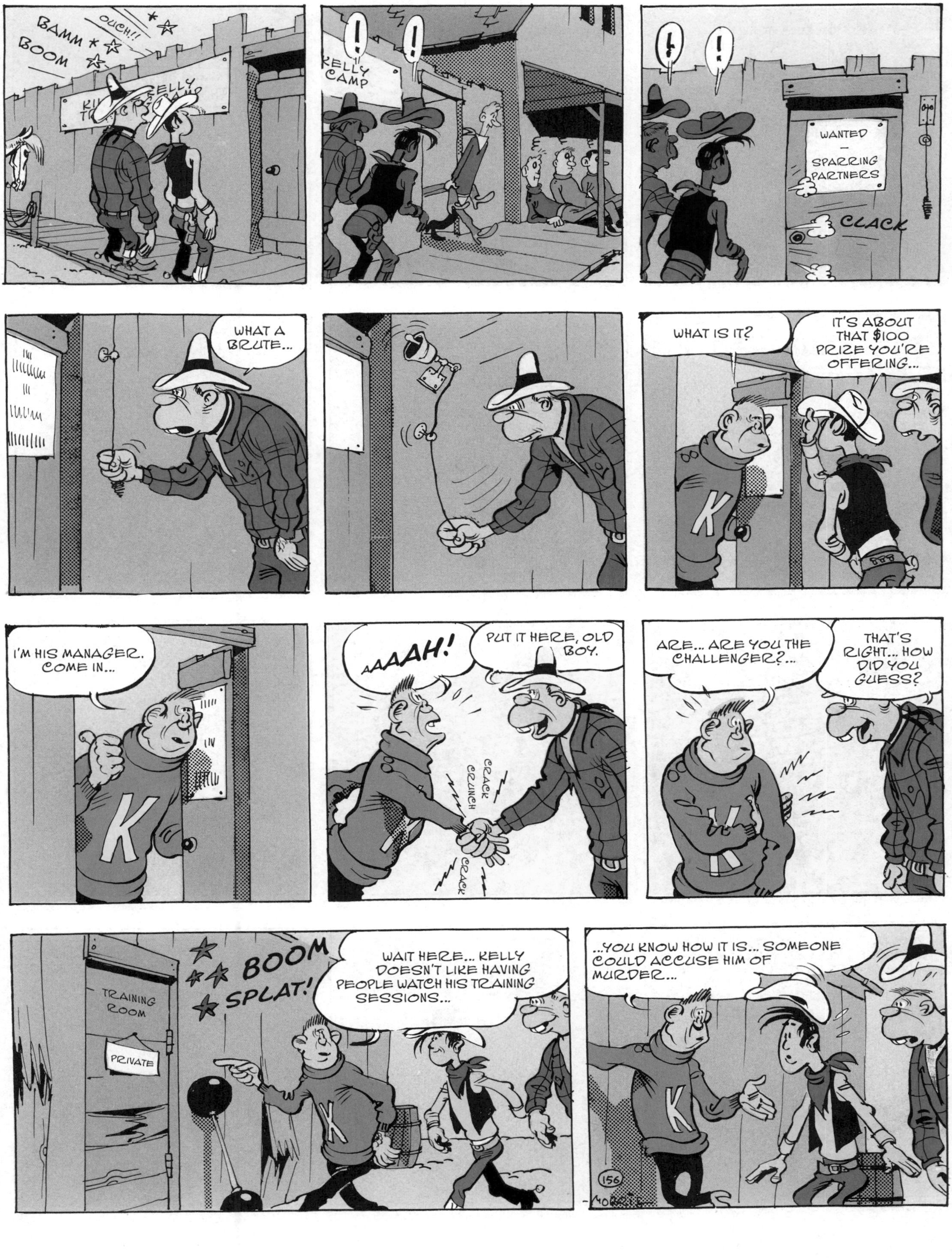
BAMM
BOOM
OUCH!!
KELLY CAMP
!
!
WANTED — SPARRING PARTNERS
CLACK
WHAT A BRUTE...
WHAT IS IT?
IT'S ABOUT THAT $100 PRIZE YOU'RE OFFERING...
I'M HIS MANAGER. COME IN...
AAAAH!
PUT IT HERE, OLD BOY.
CRACK
CRUNCH
CRACK
ARE... ARE YOU THE CHALLENGER?...
THAT'S RIGHT... HOW DID YOU GUESS?
BOOM
SPLAT!
TRAINING ROOM
PRIVATE
WAIT HERE... KELLY DOESN'T LIKE HAVING PEOPLE WATCH HIS TRAINING SESSIONS...
...YOU KNOW HOW IT IS... SOMEONE COULD ACCUSE HIM OF MURDER...

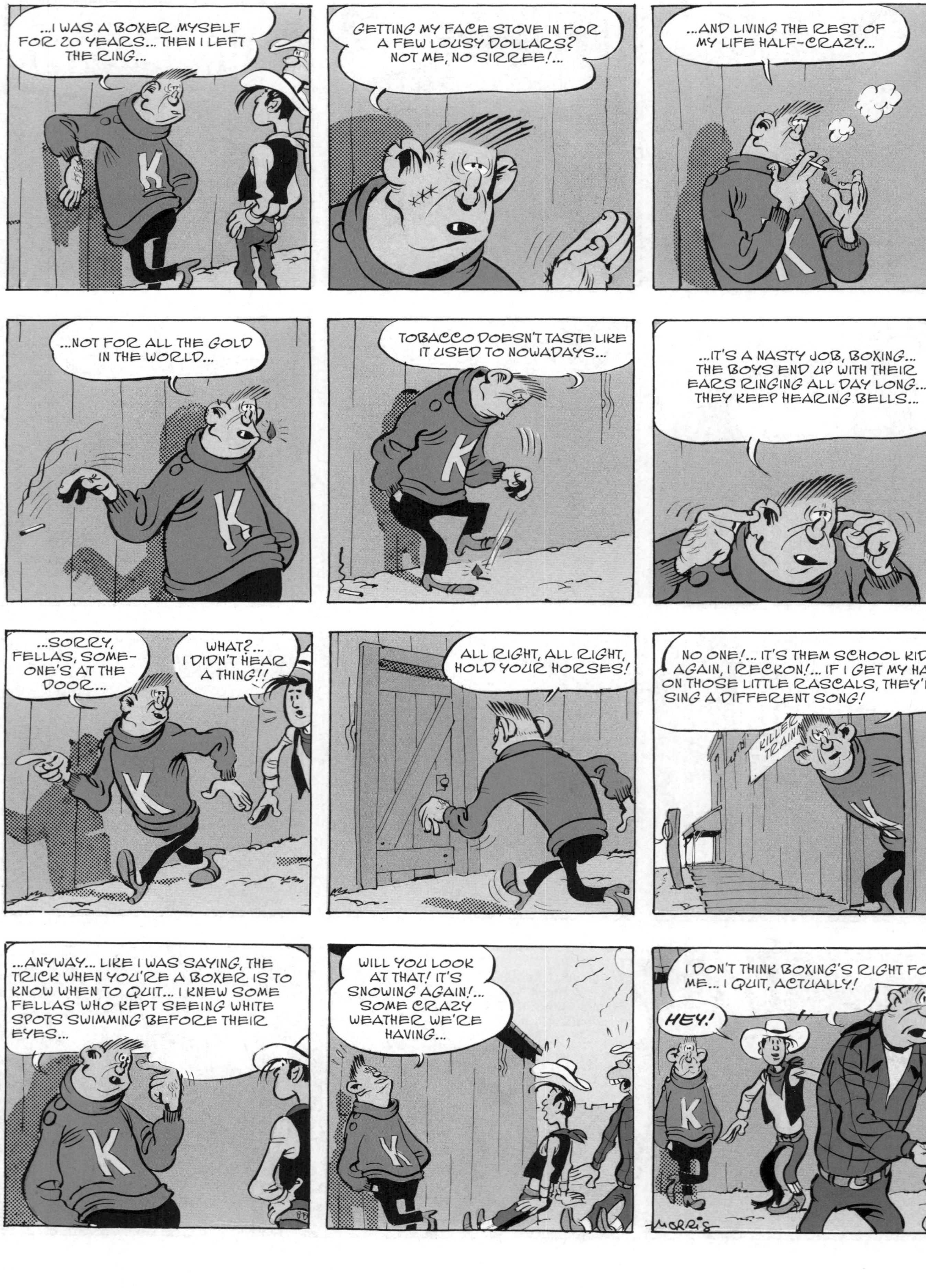

...I WAS A BOXER MYSELF FOR 20 YEARS... THEN I LEFT THE RING...
GETTING MY FACE STOVE IN FOR A FEW LOUSY DOLLARS? NOT ME, NO SIRREE!...
...AND LIVING THE REST OF MY LIFE HALF-CRAZY...
...NOT FOR ALL THE GOLD IN THE WORLD...
TOBACCO DOESN'T TASTE LIKE IT USED TO NOWADAYS...
...IT'S A NASTY JOB, BOXING... THE BOYS END UP WITH THEIR EARS RINGING ALL DAY LONG... THEY KEEP HEARING BELLS...
...SORRY, FELLAS, SOME-ONE'S AT THE DOOR...
WHAT?... I DIDN'T HEAR A THING!!
ALL RIGHT, ALL RIGHT, HOLD YOUR HORSES!
NO ONE!... IT'S THEM SCHOOL KIDS AGAIN, I RECKON!... IF I GET MY HAND ON THOSE LITTLE RASCALS, THEY'LL SING A DIFFERENT SONG!
KILLER TRAIN
...ANYWAY... LIKE I WAS SAYING, THE TRICK WHEN YOU'RE A BOXER IS TO KNOW WHEN TO QUIT... I KNEW SOME FELLAS WHO KEPT SEEING WHITE SPOTS SWIMMING BEFORE THEIR EYES...
WILL YOU LOOK AT THAT! IT'S SNOWING AGAIN!... SOME CRAZY WEATHER WE'RE HAVING...
I DON'T THINK BOXING'S RIGHT FOR ME... I QUIT, ACTUALLY!
HEY!
MORRIS
157

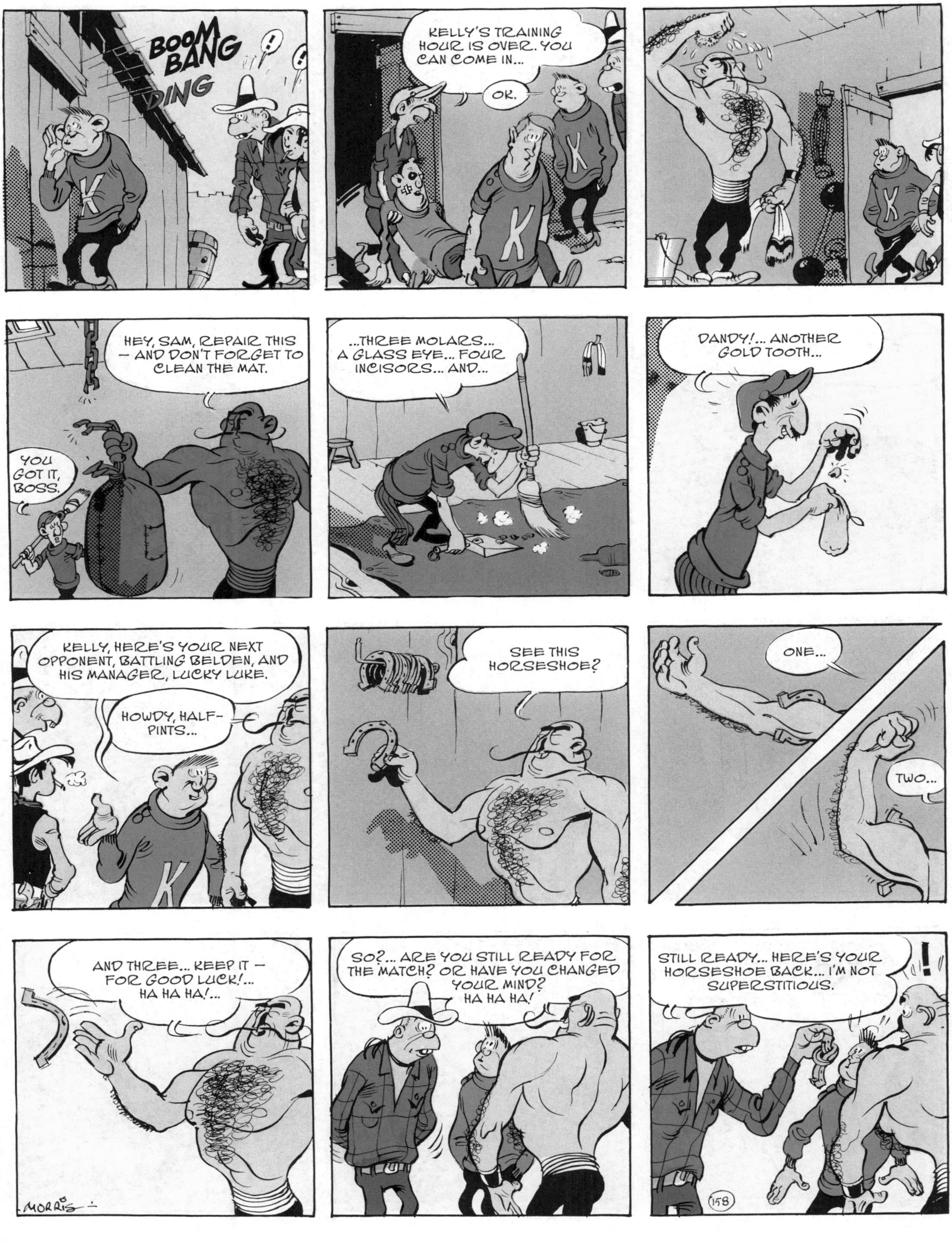
BOOM
BANG
DING
!
!
KELLY'S TRAINING HOUR IS OVER. YOU CAN COME IN...
OK.
HEY, SAM, REPAIR THIS – AND DON'T FORGET TO CLEAN THE MAT.
YOU GOT IT, BOSS.
...THREE MOLARS... A GLASS EYE... FOUR INCISORS... AND...
DANDY!... ANOTHER GOLD TOOTH...
KELLY, HERE'S YOUR NEXT OPPONENT, BATTLING BELDEN, AND HIS MANAGER, LUCKY LUKE.
HOWDY, HALF-PINTS...
SEE THIS HORSESHOE?
ONE...
TWO...
AND THREE... KEEP IT – FOR GOOD LUCK!... HA HA HA!...
MORRIS
SO?... ARE YOU STILL READY FOR THE MATCH? OR HAVE YOU CHANGED YOUR MIND? HA HA HA!
STILL READY... HERE'S YOUR HORSESHOE BACK... I'M NOT SUPERSTITIOUS.
!
158

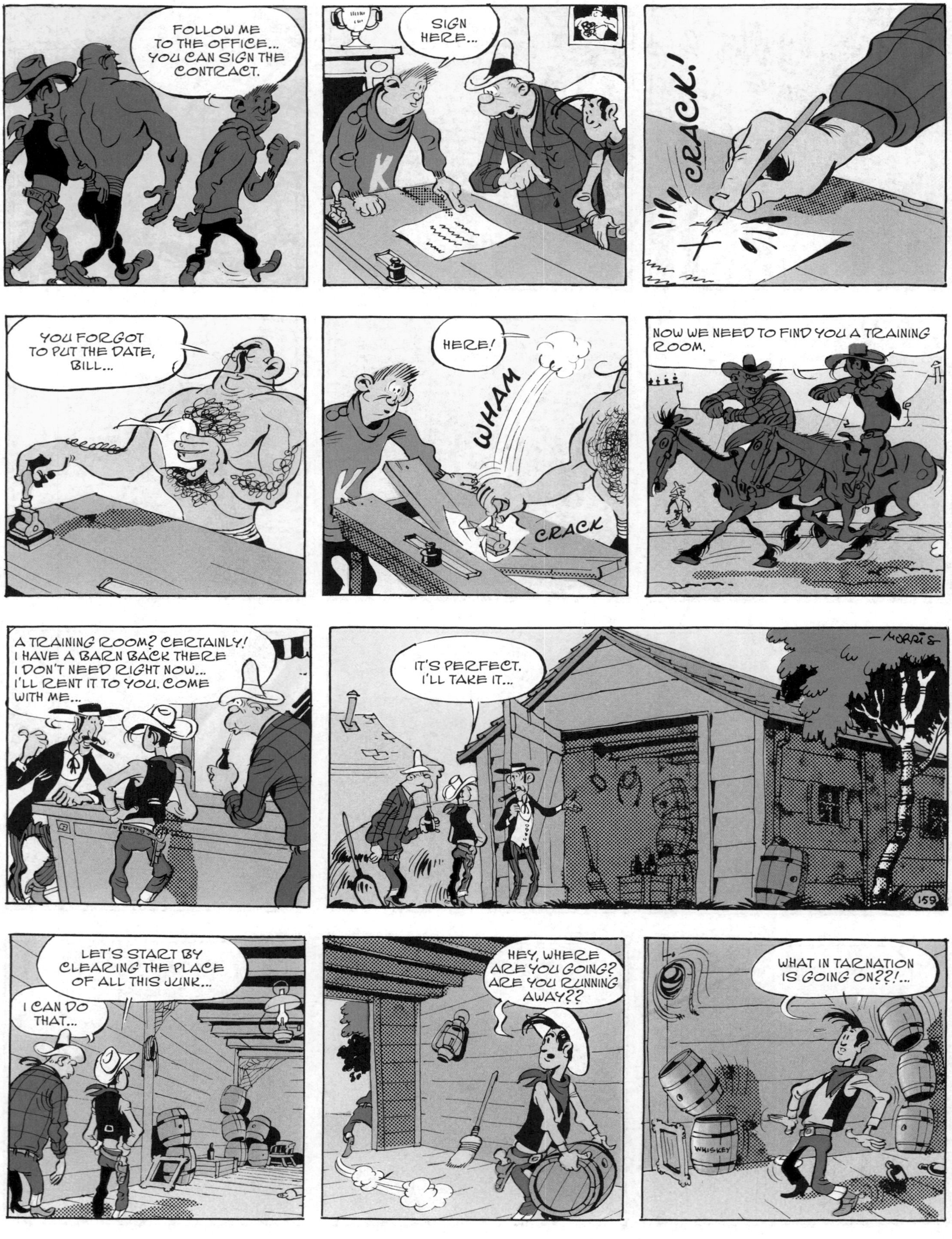
FOLLOW ME TO THE OFFICE... YOU CAN SIGN THE CONTRACT.
SIGN HERE...
CRACK!
YOU FORGOT TO PUT THE DATE, BILL...
HERE!
WHAM
CRACK
NOW WE NEED TO FIND YOU A TRAINING ROOM.
A TRAINING ROOM? CERTAINLY! I HAVE A BARN BACK THERE I DON'T NEED RIGHT NOW... I'LL RENT IT TO YOU. COME WITH ME...
IT'S PERFECT. I'LL TAKE IT...
MORRIS
LET'S START BY CLEARING THE PLACE OF ALL THIS JUNK...
I CAN DO THAT...
HEY, WHERE ARE YOU GOING? ARE YOU RUNNING AWAY??
WHAT IN TARNATION IS GOING ON??!...
WHISKEY

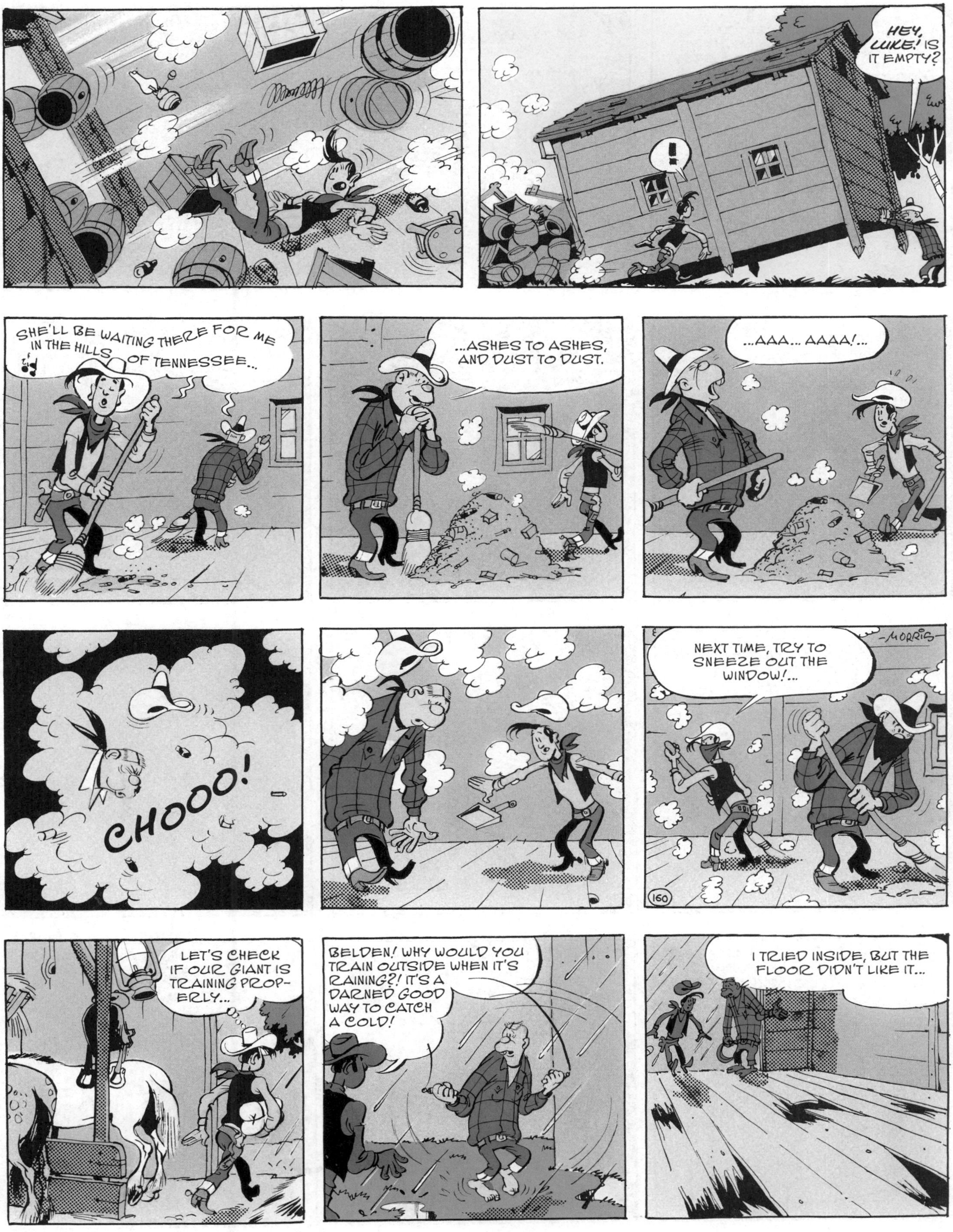
HEY, LUKE! IS IT EMPTY?
!
SHE'LL BE WAITING THERE FOR ME IN THE HILLS OF TENNESSEE...
...ASHES TO ASHES, AND DUST TO DUST.
...AAA... AAAA!...
CHOOO!
-MORRIS
NEXT TIME, TRY TO SNEEZE OUT THE WINDOW!...
160
LET'S CHECK IF OUR GIANT IS TRAINING PROP-ERLY...
BELDEN! WHY WOULD YOU TRAIN OUTSIDE WHEN IT'S RAINING?! IT'S A DARNED GOOD WAY TO CATCH A COLD!
I TRIED INSIDE, BUT THE FLOOR DIDN'T LIKE IT...

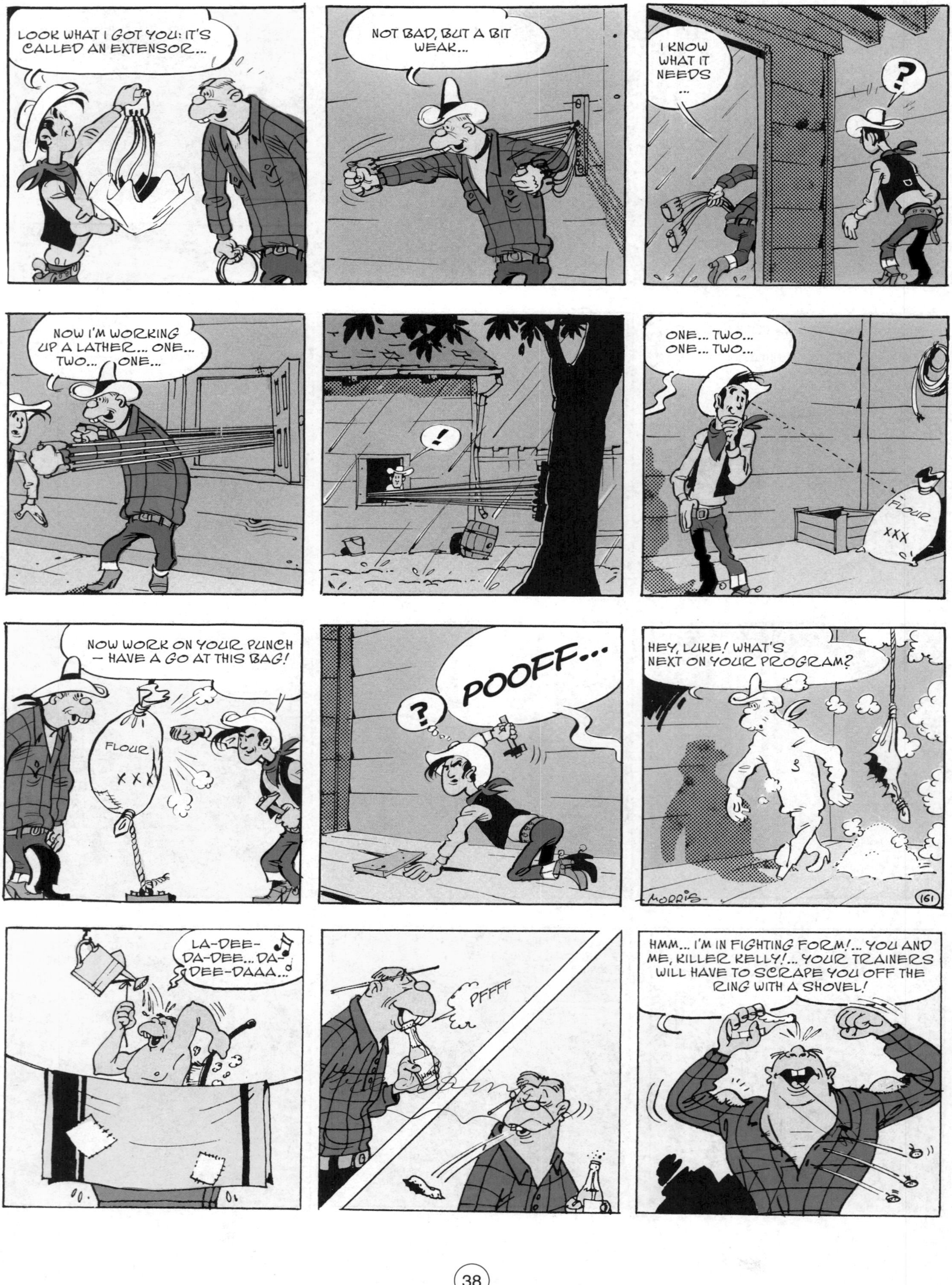
LOOK WHAT I GOT YOU: IT'S CALLED AN EXTENSOR...
NOT BAD, BUT A BIT WEAK...
I KNOW WHAT IT NEEDS ...
?
NOW I'M WORKING UP A LATHER... ONE... TWO... ONE...
!
ONE... TWO... ONE... TWO...
FLOUR
XXX
NOW WORK ON YOUR PUNCH – HAVE A GO AT THIS BAG!
FLOUR
XXX
?
POOFF...
HEY, LUKE! WHAT'S NEXT ON YOUR PROGRAM?
MORRIS
161
LA-DEE-DA-DEE... DA-DEE-DAAA...
PFFFF
HMM... I'M IN FIGHTING FORM!... YOU AND ME, KILLER KELLY!... YOUR TRAINERS WILL HAVE TO SCRAPE YOU OFF THE RING WITH A SHOVEL!

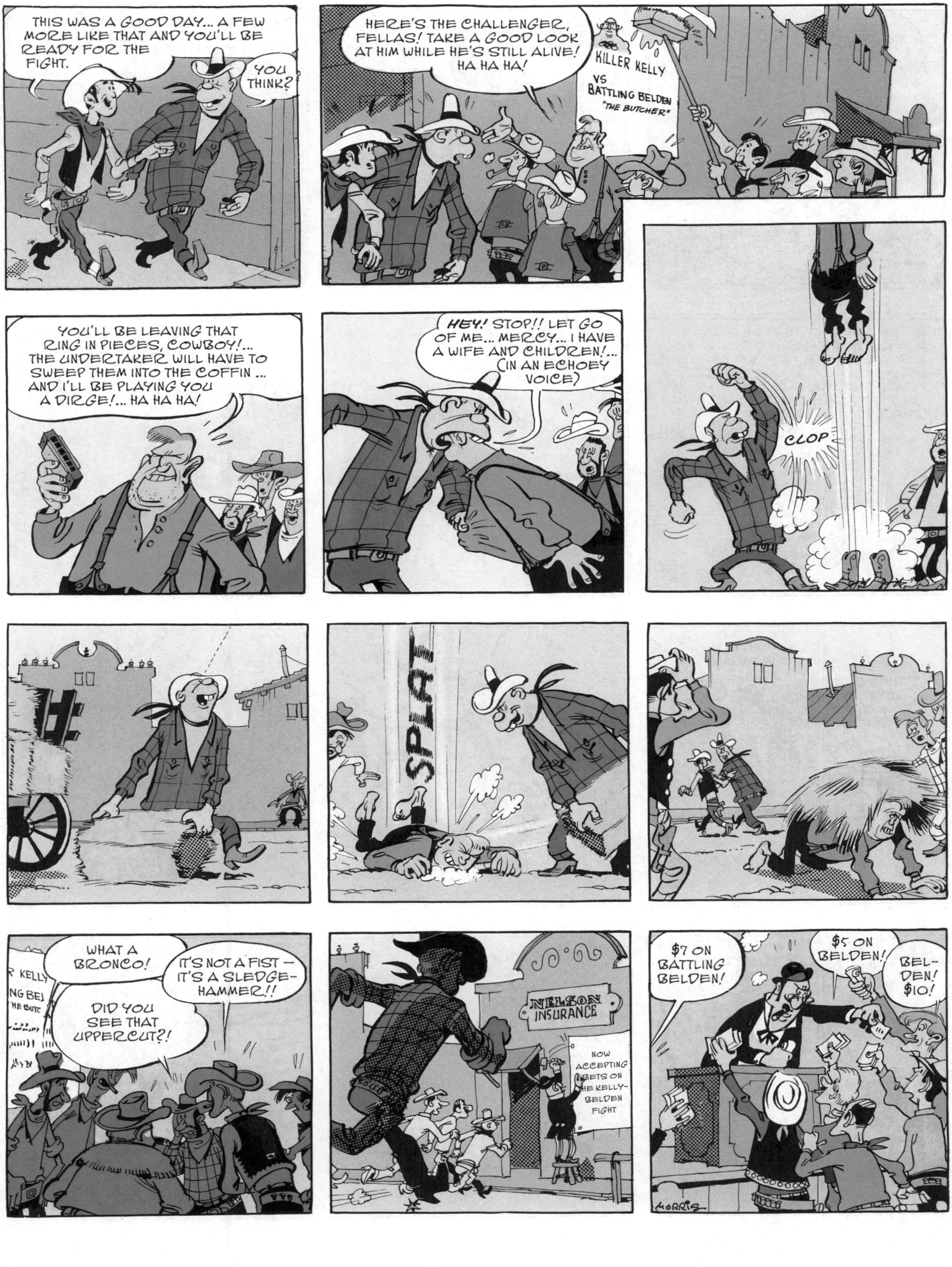
THIS WAS A GOOD DAY... A FEW MORE LIKE THAT AND YOU'LL BE READY FOR THE FIGHT.
YOU THINK?
HERE'S THE CHALLENGER, FELLAS! TAKE A GOOD LOOK AT HIM WHILE HE'S STILL ALIVE! HA HA HA!
KILLER KELLY VS BATTLING BELDEN "THE BUTCHER"
YOU'LL BE LEAVING THAT RING IN PIECES, COWBOY!... THE UNDERTAKER WILL HAVE TO SWEEP THEM INTO THE COFFIN ... AND I'LL BE PLAYING YOU A DIRGE!... HA HA HA!
HEY! STOP!! LET GO OF ME... MERCY... I HAVE A WIFE AND CHILDREN!... (IN AN ECHOEY VOICE)
CLOP
SPLAT
WHAT A BRONCO!
IT'S NOT A FIST – IT'S A SLEDGE-HAMMER!!
DID YOU SEE THAT UPPERCUT?!
NELSON INSURANCE
NOW ACCEPTING BETS ON THE KELLY-BELDEN FIGHT
$7 ON BATTLING BELDEN!
$5 ON BELDEN!
BEL-DEN! $10!
MORRIS

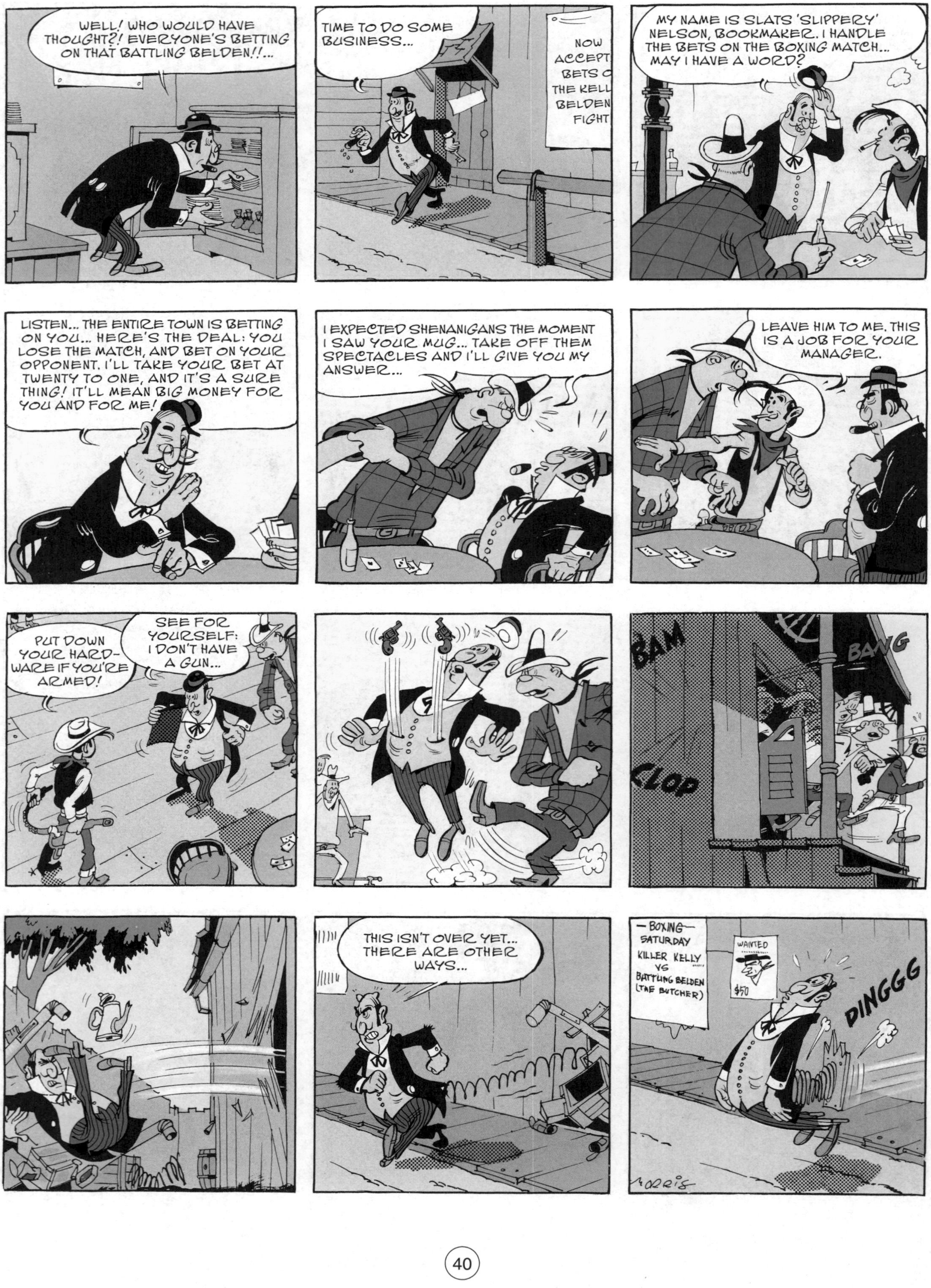
WELL! WHO WOULD HAVE THOUGHT?! EVERYONE'S BETTING ON THAT BATTLING BELDEN!!...
TIME TO DO SOME BUSINESS...
MY NAME IS SLATS 'SLIPPERY' NELSON, BOOKMAKER. I HANDLE THE BETS ON THE BOXING MATCH... MAY I HAVE A WORD?
LISTEN... THE ENTIRE TOWN IS BETTING ON YOU... HERE'S THE DEAL: YOU LOSE THE MATCH, AND BET ON YOUR OPPONENT. I'LL TAKE YOUR BET AT TWENTY TO ONE, AND IT'S A SURE THING! IT'LL MEAN BIG MONEY FOR YOU AND FOR ME!
I EXPECTED SHENANIGANS THE MOMENT I SAW YOUR MUG... TAKE OFF THEM SPECTACLES AND I'LL GIVE YOU MY ANSWER...
LEAVE HIM TO ME. THIS IS A JOB FOR YOUR MANAGER.
PUT DOWN YOUR HARD-WARE IF YOU'RE ARMED!
SEE FOR YOURSELF: I DON'T HAVE A GUN...
BAM
BANG
CLOP
THIS ISN'T OVER YET... THERE ARE OTHER WAYS...
— BOXING —
SATURDAY
KILLER KELLY
VS
BATTLING BELDEN
(THE BUTCHER)
WANTED
$50
DINGGG
MORRIS

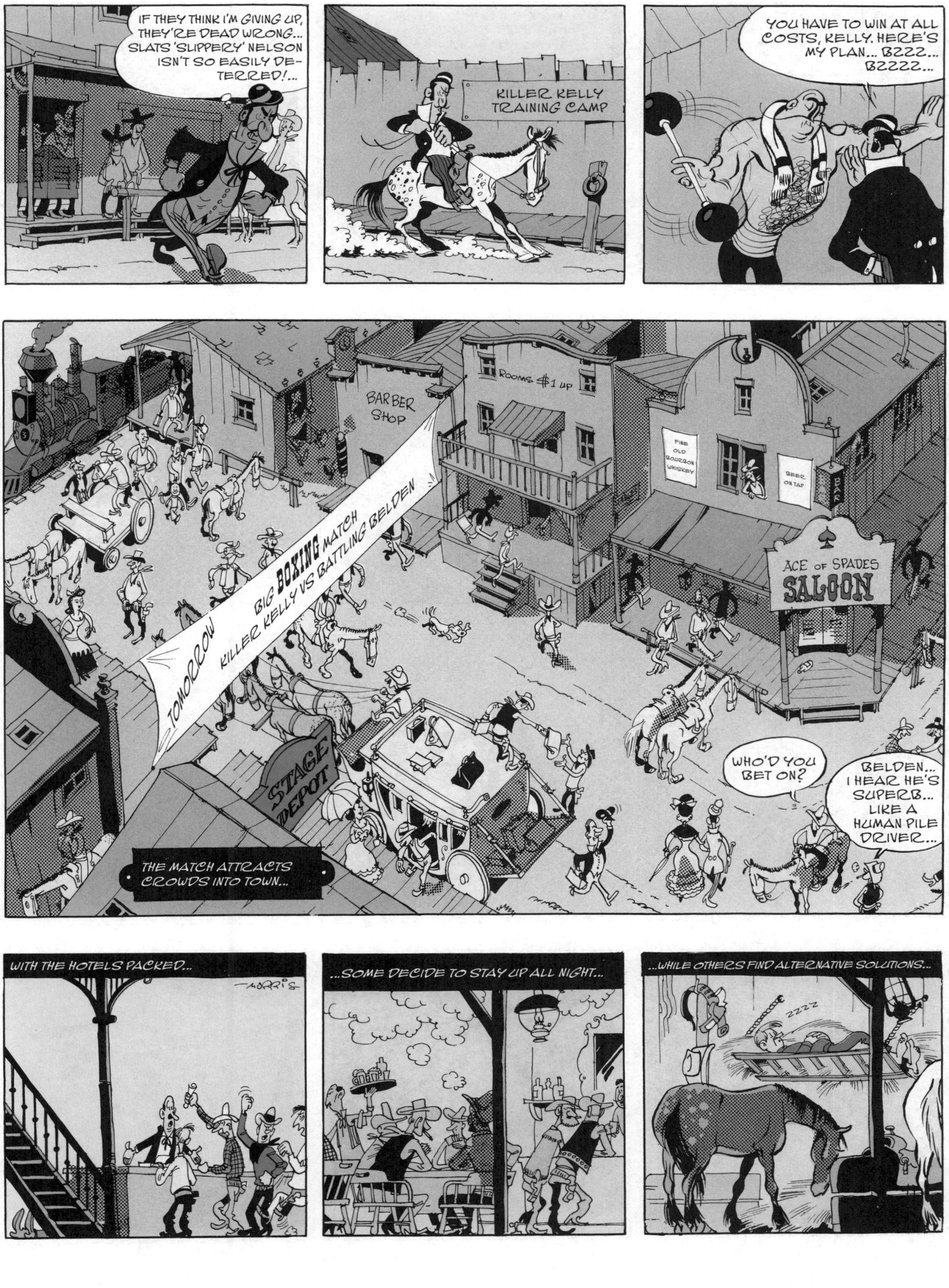
IF THEY THINK I'M GIVING UP, THEY'RE DEAD WRONG... SLATS 'SLIPPERY' NELSON ISN'T SO EASILY DE-TERRED!...
KILLER KELLY TRAINING CAMP
YOU HAVE TO WIN AT ALL COSTS, KELLY. HERE'S MY PLAN... BZZZ... BZZZZ...
BARBER SHOP
Rooms $1 up
FINE OLD BOURBON WHISKEY
BEER ON TAP
BAR
TOMORROW BIG BOXING MATCH KILLER KELLY VS BATTLING BELDEN
ACE OF SPADES SALOON
STAGE DEPOT
WHO'D YOU BET ON?
BELDEN... I HEAR HE'S SUPERB... LIKE A HUMAN PILE DRIVER...
THE MATCH ATTRACTS CROWDS INTO TOWN...
WITH THE HOTELS PACKED...
MORRIS
...SOME DECIDE TO STAY UP ALL NIGHT...
...WHILE OTHERS FIND ALTERNATIVE SOLUTIONS...
ZZZZ

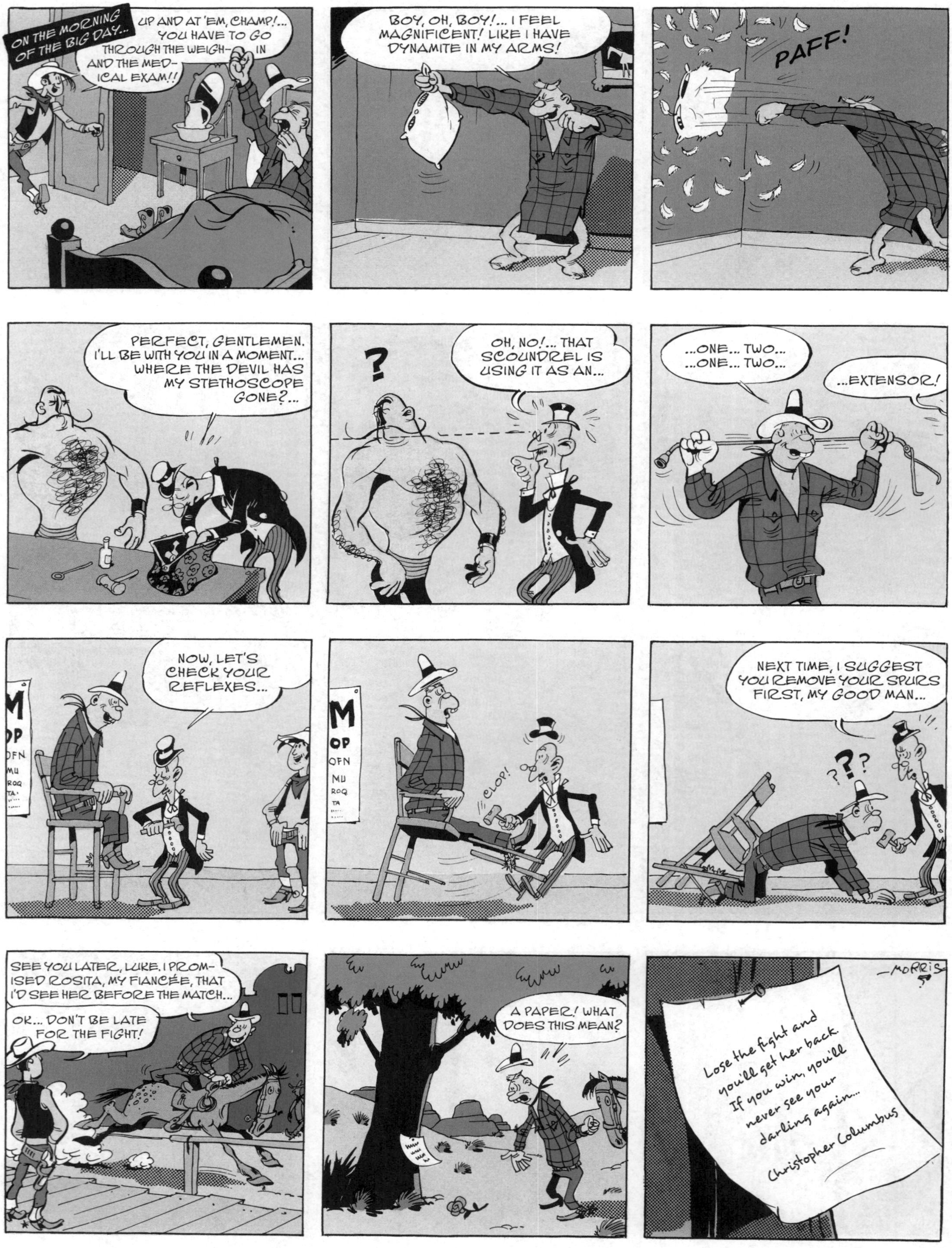
ON THE MORNING OF THE BIG DAY...
UP AND AT 'EM, CHAMP!... YOU HAVE TO GO THROUGH THE WEIGH-IN AND THE MEDICAL EXAM!!
BOY, OH, BOY!... I FEEL MAGNIFICENT! LIKE I HAVE DYNAMITE IN MY ARMS!
PAFF!
PERFECT, GENTLEMEN. I'LL BE WITH YOU IN A MOMENT... WHERE THE DEVIL HAS MY STETHOSCOPE GONE?...
?
OH, NO!... THAT SCOUNDREL IS USING IT AS AN...
...ONE... TWO... ...ONE... TWO...
...EXTENSOR!
NOW, LET'S CHECK YOUR REFLEXES...
CLOP!
NEXT TIME, I SUGGEST YOU REMOVE YOUR SPURS FIRST, MY GOOD MAN...
???
SEE YOU LATER, LUKE. I PROMISED ROSITA, MY FIANCÉE, THAT I'D SEE HER BEFORE THE MATCH...
OK... DON'T BE LATE FOR THE FIGHT!
A PAPER! WHAT DOES THIS MEAN?
MORRIS
Lose the fight and you'll get her back. If you win, you'll never see your darling again...
Christopher Columbus

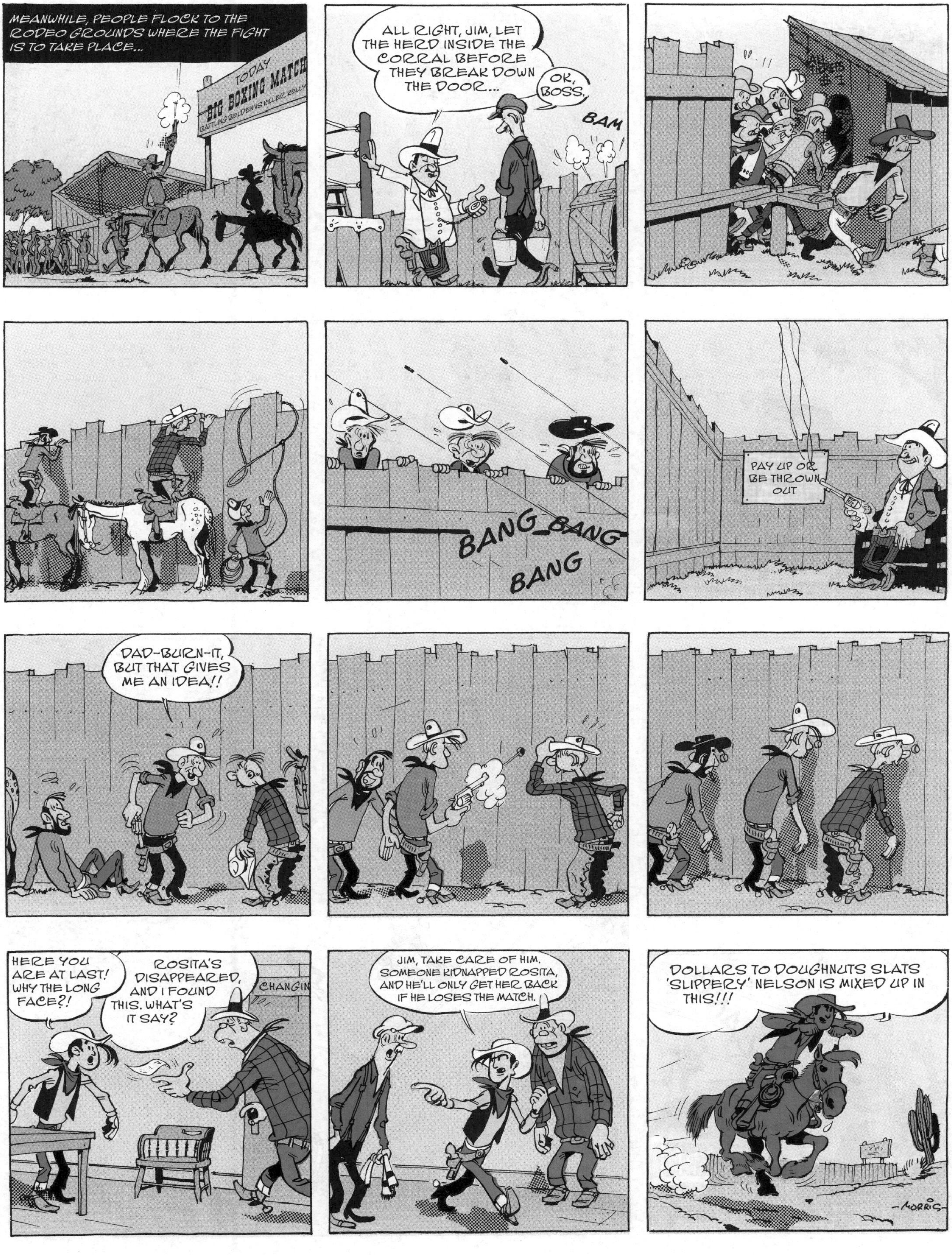
MEANWHILE, PEOPLE FLOCK TO THE RODEO GROUNDS WHERE THE FIGHT IS TO TAKE PLACE...
TODAY
BIG BOXING MATCH
BATTLING BELDEN VS KILLER KELLY
ALL RIGHT, JIM, LET THE HERD INSIDE THE CORRAL BEFORE THEY BREAK DOWN THE DOOR...
OK, BOSS.
BAM
BANG BANG
BANG
PAY UP OR BE THROWN OUT
DAD-BURN-IT, BUT THAT GIVES ME AN IDEA!!
HERE YOU ARE AT LAST! WHY THE LONG FACE?!
ROSITA'S DISAPPEARED, AND I FOUND THIS. WHAT'S IT SAY?
CHANGIN
JIM, TAKE CARE OF HIM. SOMEONE KIDNAPPED ROSITA, AND HE'LL ONLY GET HER BACK IF HE LOSES THE MATCH.
DOLLARS TO DOUGHNUTS SLATS 'SLIPPERY' NELSON IS MIXED UP IN THIS!!!
-MORRIS-

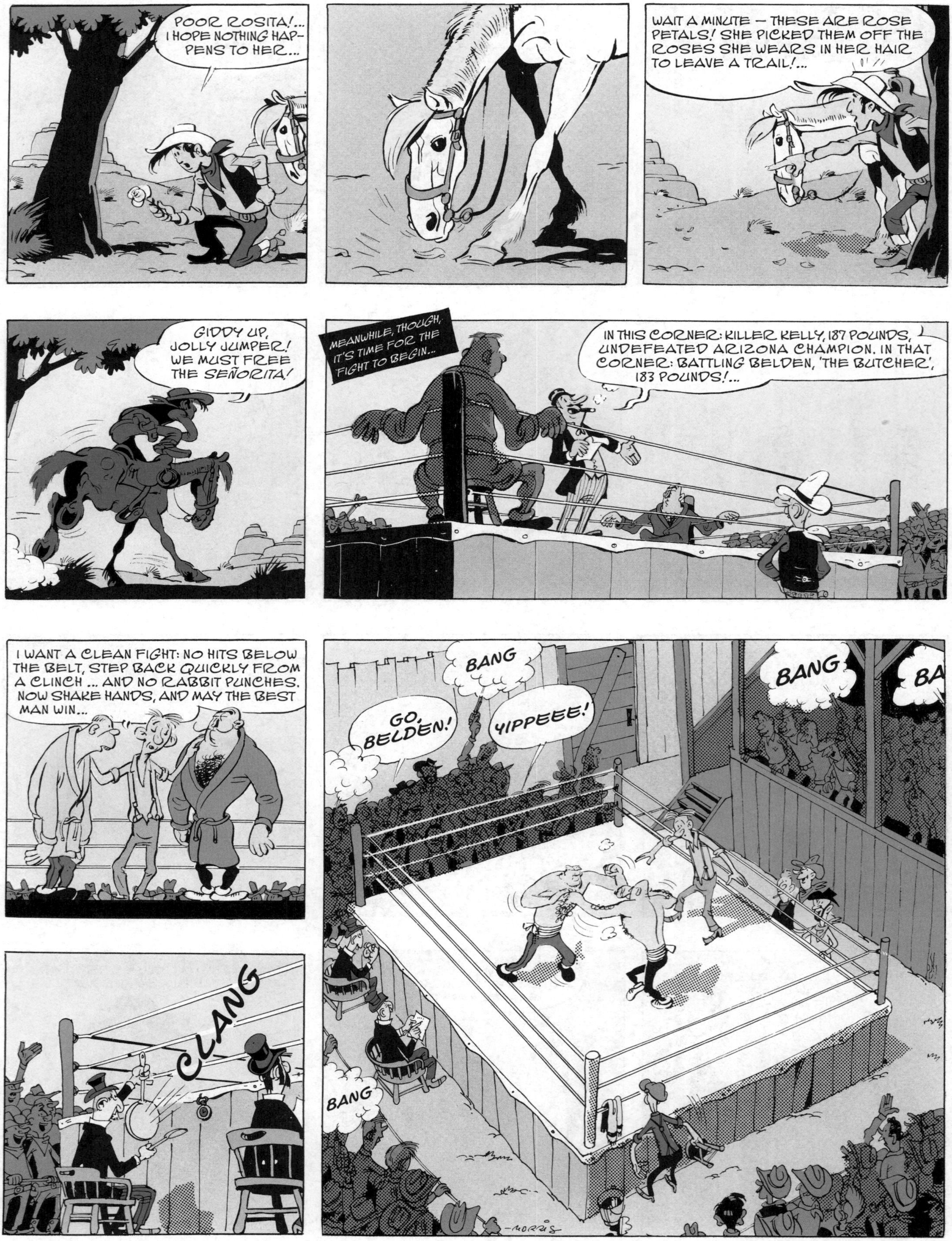
POOR ROSITA!... I HOPE NOTHING HAPPENS TO HER...
WAIT A MINUTE — THESE ARE ROSE PETALS! SHE PICKED THEM OFF THE ROSES SHE WEARS IN HER HAIR TO LEAVE A TRAIL!...
GIDDY UP, JOLLY JUMPER! WE MUST FREE THE SEÑORITA!
MEANWHILE, THOUGH, IT'S TIME FOR THE FIGHT TO BEGIN...
IN THIS CORNER: KILLER KELLY, 187 POUNDS, UNDEFEATED ARIZONA CHAMPION. IN THAT CORNER: BATTLING BELDEN, 'THE BUTCHER', 183 POUNDS!...
I WANT A CLEAN FIGHT: NO HITS BELOW THE BELT, STEP BACK QUICKLY FROM A CLINCH ... AND NO RABBIT PUNCHES. NOW SHAKE HANDS, AND MAY THE BEST MAN WIN...
CLANG
BANG
GO, BELDEN!
YIPPEEE!
BANG
BANG
MORRIS

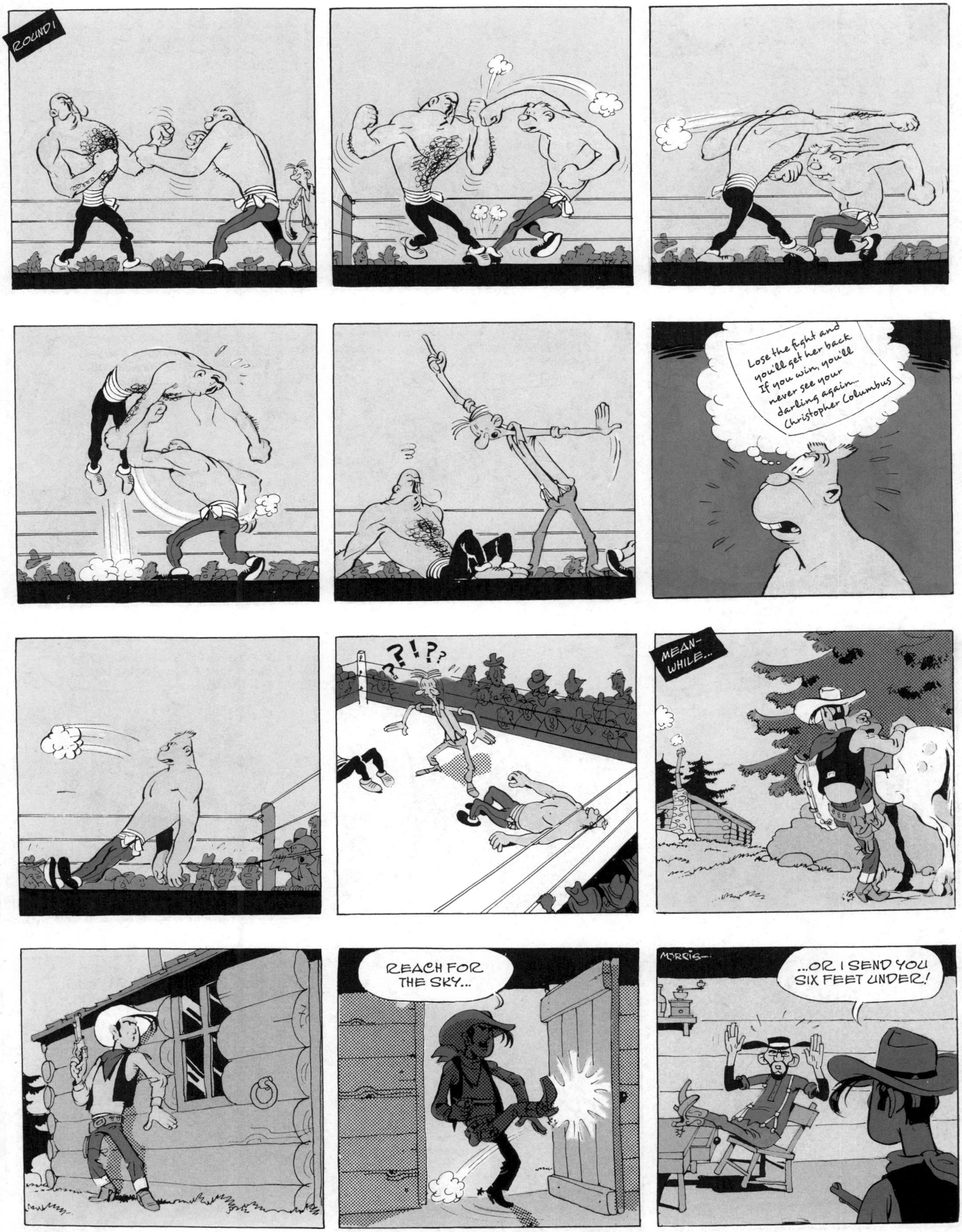
ROUND 1
Lose the fight and you'll get her back. If you win, you'll never see your darling again... Christopher Columbus
?!?
MEAN-WHILE...
MORRIS
REACH FOR THE SKY...
...OR I SEND YOU SIX FEET UNDER!

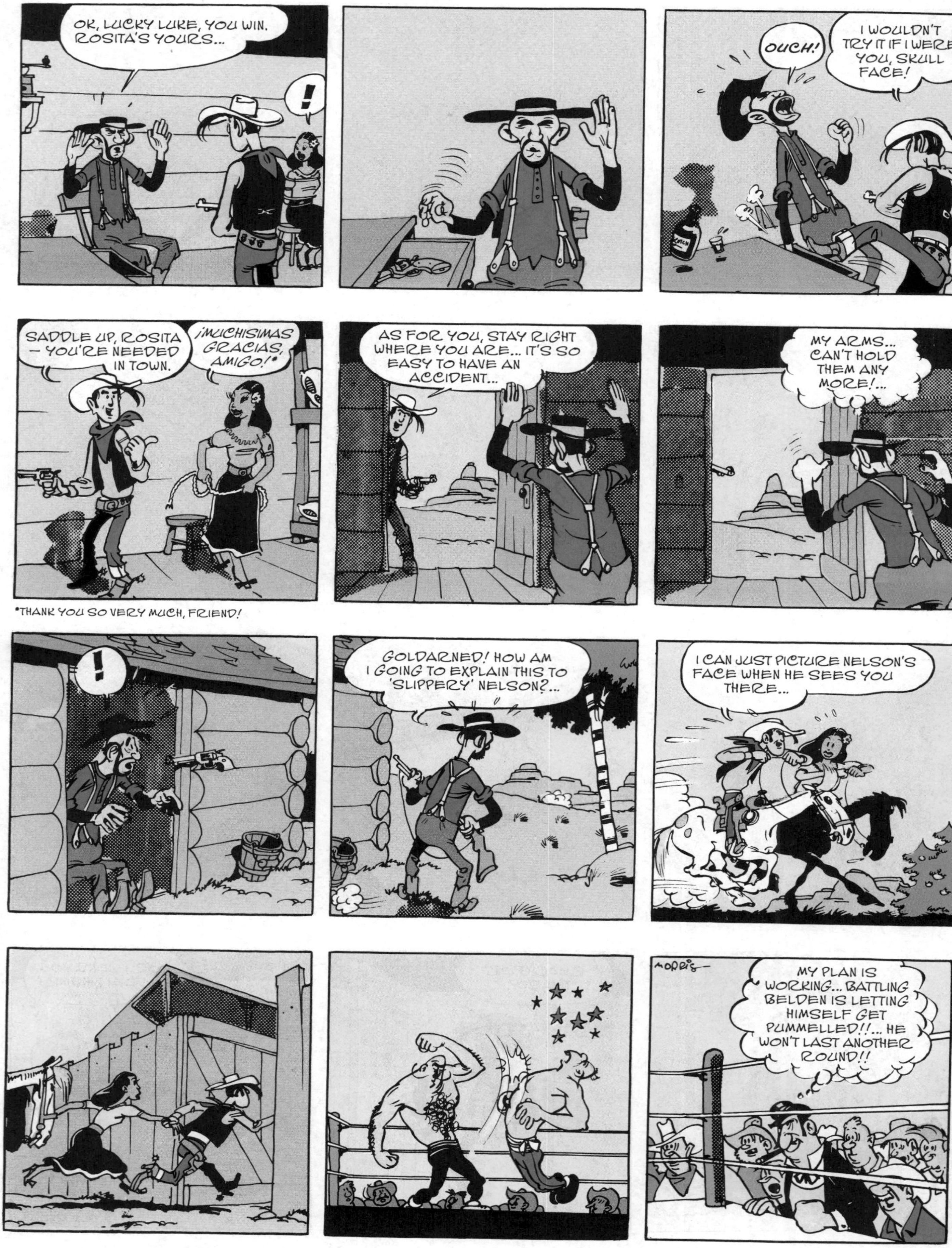
OK, LUCKY LUKE, YOU WIN. ROSITA'S YOURS...
!
OUCH!
I WOULDN'T TRY IT IF I WERE YOU, SKULL FACE!
SADDLE UP, ROSITA – YOU'RE NEEDED IN TOWN.
¡MUCHISIMAS GRACIAS, AMIGO!*
AS FOR YOU, STAY RIGHT WHERE YOU ARE... IT'S SO EASY TO HAVE AN ACCIDENT...
MY ARMS... CAN'T HOLD THEM ANY MORE!...
*THANK YOU SO VERY MUCH, FRIEND!
!
GOLDARNED! HOW AM I GOING TO EXPLAIN THIS TO 'SLIPPERY' NELSON?...
I CAN JUST PICTURE NELSON'S FACE WHEN HE SEES YOU THERE...
MY PLAN IS WORKING... BATTLING BELDEN IS LETTING HIMSELF GET PUMMELLED!!... HE WON'T LAST ANOTHER ROUND!!

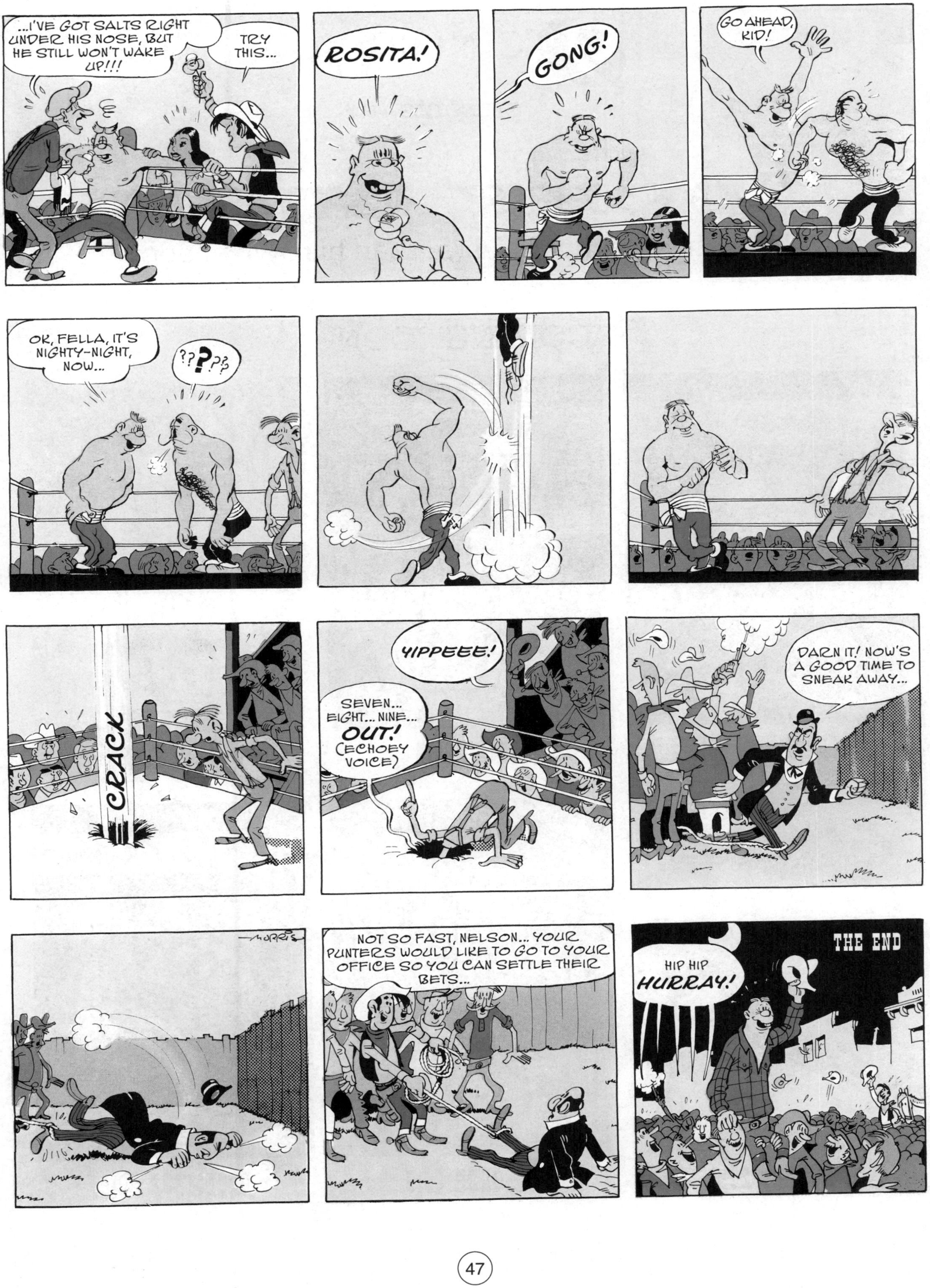
...I'VE GOT SALTS RIGHT UNDER HIS NOSE, BUT HE STILL WON'T WAKE UP!!!
TRY THIS...
ROSITA!
GONG!
GO AHEAD, KID!
OK, FELLA, IT'S NIGHTY-NIGHT, NOW...
??? ???
CRACK
YIPPEEE!
SEVEN... EIGHT... NINE... OUT! (ECHOEY VOICE)
DARN IT! NOW'S A GOOD TIME TO SNEAK AWAY...
MORRIS
NOT SO FAST, NELSON... YOUR PUNTERS WOULD LIKE TO GO TO YOUR OFFICE SO YOU CAN SETTLE THEIR BETS...
HIP HIP HURRAY!
THE END

9th CINEBOOK
The 9th Art Publisher

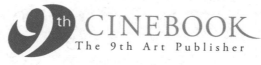

presents

LUCKY LUKE

The man who shoots faster than his own shadow

COMING SOON

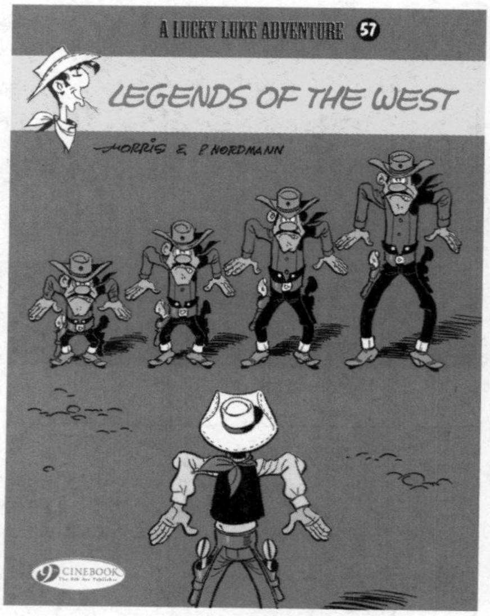

A LUCKY LUKE ADVENTURE 57
LEGENDS OF THE WEST
MORRIS & P. NORDMANN
CINEBOOK

FEBRUARY 2016

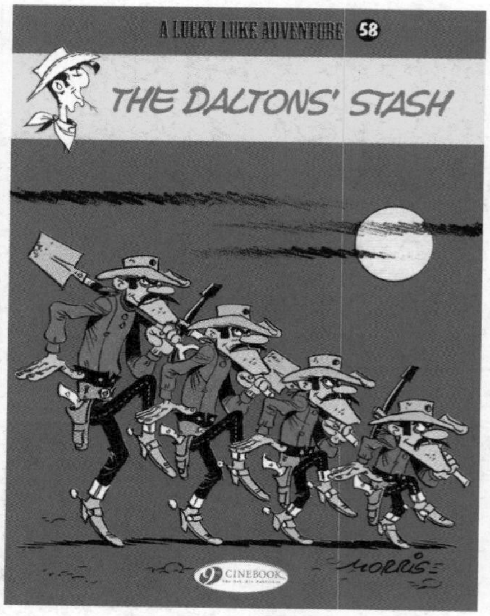

A LUCKY LUKE ADVENTURE 58
THE DALTONS' STASH
MORRIS
CINEBOOK

APRIL 2016

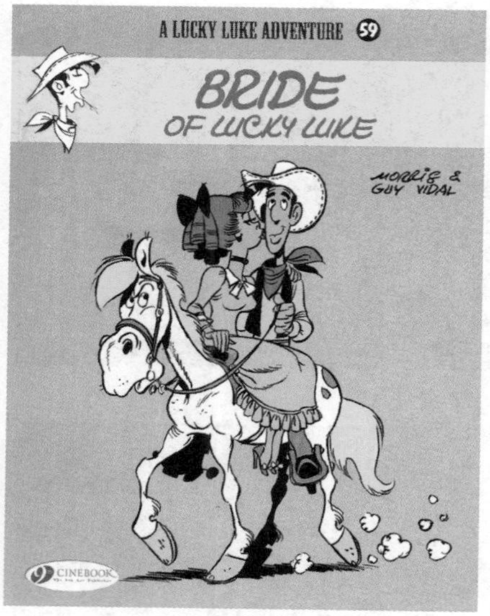

A LUCKY LUKE ADVENTURE 59
BRIDE
OF LUCKY LUKE
MORRIS &
GUY VIDAL
CINEBOOK

JUNE 2016

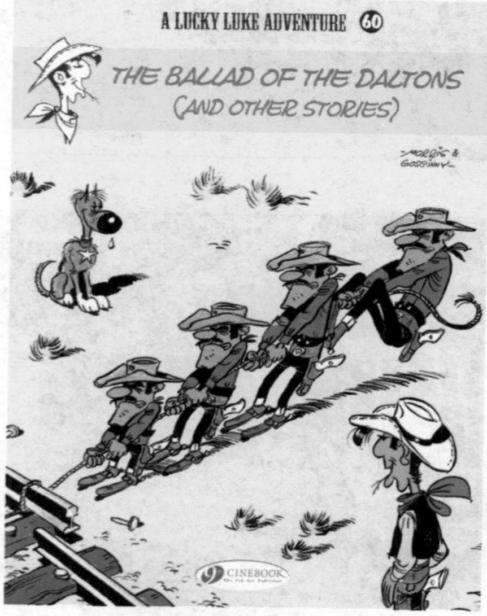

A LUCKY LUKE ADVENTURE 60
THE BALLAD OF THE DALTONS
(AND OTHER STORIES)
MORRIS &
GOSCINNY
CINEBOOK

AUGUST 2016

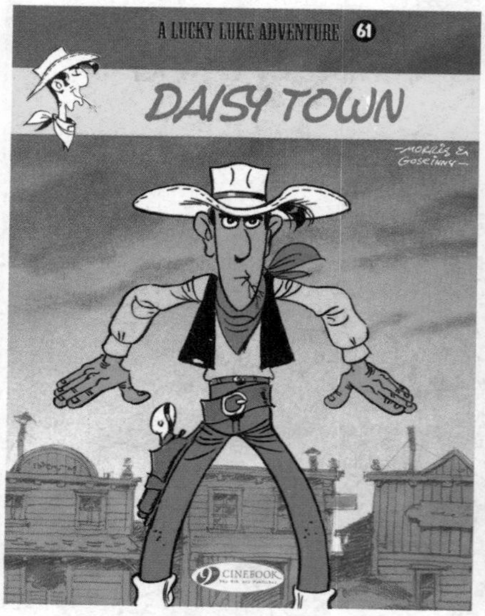

A LUCKY LUKE ADVENTURE 61
DAISY TOWN
MORRIS &
GOSCINNY
CINEBOOK

OCTOBER 2016

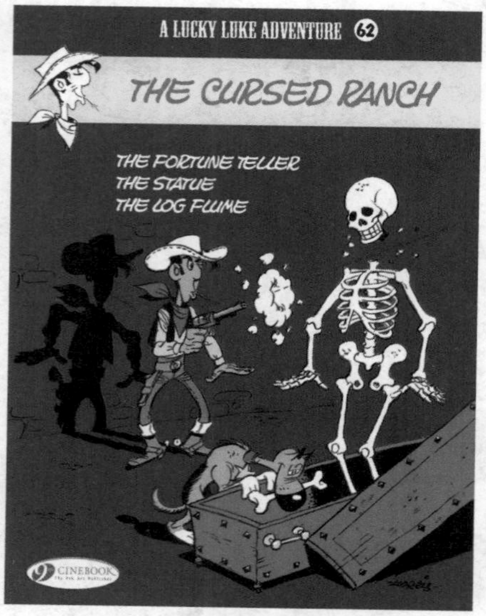

A LUCKY LUKE ADVENTURE 62
THE CURSED RANCH
THE FORTUNE TELLER
THE STATUE
THE LOG FLUME
CINEBOOK

DECEMBER 2016